"I'm Sick Of Being Told Who And What I Am!

"And what I really want," Connie told Jud in a choked voice. "I'm not the lovestruck nineteen-year-old my ex-husband could manipulate at will, and I'm not the spoiled incompetent you seem to take me for. I can do anything anybody else can, and more than some. And if you, Judson Halverson, are too pigheaded to admit that, then don't come around and bother me anymore."

Jud took two long steps to grip Connie's shoulders. "The man said he loves you, and that he wants to make amends—"

"He wants to use me! He's cheated and betrayed me at every turn. How can you think he loves me?"

Jud closed his eyes and pulled her into his arms. He laid his cheek against her hair and asked softly, "How can he not?"

Dear Reader:

I hope you've been enjoying 1989, our "Year of the Man" at Silhouette Desire. Every one of the twelve authors who are contributing a *Man of the Month* has created a very special someone for your reading pleasure. Each man is unique, and each author's style and characterization give you a different insight into her man's story.

From January to December, 1989 will be a twelve-month extravaganza spotlighting one book each month with special cover treatment as a tribute to the Silhouette Desire hero—our *Man of the Month*!

Created by your favorite authors, these men are utterly irresistible. Love, betrayal, greed and revenge are all part of Lucy Gordon's dramatic *Vengeance Is Mine*, featuring Luke Harmon as Mr. May, and I think you'll find Annette Broadrick's Quinn McNamara . . . *Irresistible*! Coming in June.

Don't let these men get away!

Yours,

Isabel Swift
Senior Editor & Editorial Coordinator

ANNE PETERS
Like Wildfire

Silhouette Desire

Published by Silhouette Books New York

America's Publisher of Contemporary Romance

SILHOUETTE BOOKS
300 East 42nd St., New York, N.Y. 10017

ISBN: 0-373-05497-1

First Silhouette Books printing May 1989

All the characters in this book are fictitious. Any
resemblance to actual persons, living or dead, is
purely coincidental.

®: Trademark used under license and
registered in the United States Patent and
Trademark Office and in other countries.

Printed in the U.S.A.

ANNE PETERS

has either lived or traveled in virtually every part of the world, but her roots are firmly planted in Pacific Northwest soil now. A mother—and grandmother—of two, she lives with her salesmanager husband in Renton, Washington. When not writing, she reads, gardens, baby-sits her grandchildren or travels—and has even been known to do housework at times.

To Jan Tatum,
native of Montana and oft-consulted friend.
To Gail Hon and Mary Anne Mauermann
who, each in her own way, made me a writer.
To "the group":
Roz, Suzie, Dorothy, Leslie and Barbara—
with gratitude and affection.
And, last but not least,
my thanks to Jerry Fineman
of the U.S. Forest Service for his time,
his courtesy and his tolerance
of my many dumb questions.

One

Constance Martinelli eased the mud-spattered Ford Bronco over yet another pothole and jerked to a halt in front of the Starbrite Motel. The engine shuddered once and stalled, as it had all too often during the twenty-four hours of her ownership.

Connie slumped behind the wheel and turned her head to intercept her passenger's fixed stare. Dark, sleek, menacingly handsome, he had a way of looking at her that made her feel inept.

"All right, so I should have disengaged the clutch," she snapped. "If you're so all-fired smart, why don't *you* drive from now on?"

Rudolph Valentino, dog that he was, barked a short reply and yawned. Then he settled more comfortably in his seat, seemingly content to watch as Connie belatedly depressed the troublesome pedal, shifted into first and set the brake.

Connie pulled the keys from the ignition and dropped them into her handbag.

"Stay," she told Rudy, opening the door and stepping smack into one of the puddles that littered the parking lot like land mines.

"Rats!"

She slammed the door shut and propped a bracing hand against it. Lifting first one foot, then the other, she contemplated her once-white, now-oozing new Nikes. *Fifty bucks shot.*

Taking a steadying breath of clear Montana air, she counted to ten, reflecting that even though Mattville now had a supermarket instead of a general store and a video-rental place where the old movie house used to be some things never changed. Like unpaved parking lots and mud puddles.

Connie sloshed to dry ground and looked around. And things like the bright pink walls of Slater's motel and the pink elephant surrounded by a burst of stars that still graced the top of the VACANCY sign with the *N* inserted backward and the apparently timeless legend WELC ME HUN ERS.

Connie shook her head in amazement. Still, in spite of her ruined shoes, she was somehow glad that was how things were—timeless, steadfast.

Wiping the saturated Nikes on the sparse tufts of grass cleaned her soles sufficiently that she didn't leave tracks when she climbed the three steps leading to a sagging porch and a door marked Office.

As she neared it, the boards vibrated beneath another tread, this one brisker and heavier. A large presence briefly eclipsed Connie's small form as a long arm and a work-gloved hand reached past her for the doorknob. A fleeting scent of horses and hay tickled her nose. A burst of warm breath fanned the fine hairs at her temple, and a deeply resonant voice spoke somewhere above her right ear.

"Allow me."

Stepping aside, Connie glanced up into eyes the color of a clear mountain stream. They met her look of startled inquiry with one of friendly courtesy as their owner pushed open the door and beckoned her inside ahead of him. A cowboy, Connie thought, noting the battered Stetson and the weathered face. Well, hardly a *boy*, she amended, guessing him to be near forty, and apparently a gentleman, in spite of the well-worn jeans and the stained work shirt. Her grandmother had always claimed that in this part of the world men knew how to treat a lady. It seemed she'd been right.

"Howdy," she ventured, choking back the word *pardner*. That might be overdoing the Western touch a bit, she decided, adding, "Nice day, isn't it?" instead. She offered a smile but made no move to enter the office.

"Very nice," the cowboy replied, amusement adding extra sparkle to the crystalline gaze that skimmed Connie's form before returning to her face. His grin was lopsided as he again motioned Connie inside. "After you, ma'am."

Ma'am. Connie stifled a laugh. The word had a nice courtly ring to it. Chivalry wasn't dead, she thought, it had merely fled from New York City and settled in Montana. And even though she firmly believed in equality between the sexes and treasured her hard-won independence she decided there was no harm in humoring this cowboy's old-fashioned manners. When in Rome...

"Thank you."

"You're surely welcome."

Connie did her best to sashay into the cramped room, swinging an imaginary skirt and bustle as she stepped over the threshhold. She paused to let her eyes adjust to the gloom and was reassured to find that here, too, the passage of time had wrought few changes. The walls were still paneled in imitation walnut, and President Eisenhower's fading likeness still hung right next to a shopworn rack of antlers. The odor of mothballs mixed with stale tobacco was pungent.

Elsie Slater, older and grayer but not an ounce thinner, sat behind an ancient desk, pounding away at a vintage Remington whose keys clacked with staccato reluctance. Looking up as they entered, her gaze rested briefly and without recognition on Connie, then warmed as it shifted beyond her to the man.

"Jud," she said by way of a greeting. "You still on vacation?"

"Yeah, if you want to call it that," the man called Jud replied, a hint of laughter roughening his mellow baritone. "I've been working my tail off clearing brush and fencing a corral over at my place. George around?"

Connie turned her head to look at the cowboy as he spoke. With his body all but pressed against hers where they stood just inside the door, his face was mere inches away. And a very nice face it was, too. Tanned, craggy and stubbled, it nevertheless conveyed strength, intelligence and pride.

In Connie's estimation, this was no ordinary cowboy. Definitely a rancher, she decided, and let her gaze roam upward from well-shaped lips to... She was caught. While speaking to Elsie, the man had been eyeing Connie with a degree of interest and appreciation that matched her own.

Their eyes locked. The wave of awareness that tingled and prickled through Connie's veins was unexpected and unsettling. She forced herself to count to three slowly before lowering her lashes with a deliberate show of nonchalance and breaking the visual contact. She was appalled by her body's reaction to this man, and she moved aside a couple of steps to create some distance between them.

She focused on Elsie, who had abandoned the typewriter and was now standing behind the reception counter. Her elbows rested on its top, and her numerous chins were supported on folded hands. "George went over to Hamilton," she was saying, her eyes darting from Jud to Connie and back again. "Did you need something?"

"Naw." Jud's drawl was of such honeyed laziness that Connie's eyes were drawn back to him in spite of her best efforts. "Just thought he might like to go fishing."

He nodded in Connie's direction and straightened away from the door. "You'd best take care of this little lady, Elsie, otherwise she's liable to run off. We wouldn't want to lose such a pretty visitor, now would we?"

Little lady? Connie winced, reminded that the "chivalry" she had so good-naturedly accepted moments before was invariably the flip side of chauvinism. About to protest, Jud cut her short by saying, "Enjoy your stay," with a wink and another of his lopsided grins.

Touching a finger to the brim of his hat, he added, "Ladies," and strode away.

Connie released the breath with which she had intended to voice her objection. Good riddance, she thought with a touch of wry annoyance. Maybe now she could get on with the business at hand. She walked up to the counter.

Elsie's gaze lingered on the empty doorway. "Somethin', ain't he?"

Connie's responding laugh was spontaneous, a release from the tension she ruefully admitted the man's presence and intent regard had caused her to feel.

"*He* certainly seems to think so," she said.

"Don't you believe it." Elsie was down off her cloud now, and defensive. "Jud's a fine man. Real fine." She studied Connie, frowning. "Say, don't I know you?"

"I'm Constance Martinelli, Mrs. Slater," Connie said, then belatedly remembered she was Constance *Jacobi* again, even if her driver's license didn't say so yet. "I came to stay with my grandparents one summer, oh, about fifteen years ago, I guess. Gram would bring me along when she'd visit with you here in town once a week. The Olsons?" she added when Elsie continued to look unenlightened.

"Olson!" Elsie Slater exclaimed, a dawning smile illuminating her face. "Of course! I remember now! You're Jake and Connie Olson's little grandkid from Chicago. I knew you looked familiar."

With a speed that was amazing for a woman her size, she rounded the counter and took Connie's hand in both of hers. "My, but it's good to see you."

Warm feelings dashed any remaining doubts Connie might have had about coming to Montana. This place, these nice people, were just what she needed after the hectic pace of her life in New York.

Connie laid her free hand on top of Elsie's and squeezed. "Thank you, Elsie. It's wonderful to be back. I loved the time I spent here."

Gently withdrawing her hands and placing them on her ample hips, Elsie backed up a step. "There now, honey, let's have a look at you. My, my, you're all grown up. What are you now, twenty-four, -five?"

"Twenty-eight."

"Twenty-eight? Don't time fly, though? Here you are, a grown woman, pretty as a picture. The spittin' image of your mama, now that I look at you, what with them golden curls and them big brown eyes—or are they green?"

Connie laughed delightedly. "Hazel."

"Yup, that'd be it." Elsie's own bright blue eyes all but disappeared in the folds of her answering smile. "How *is* your mother?"

"Fine, last I heard. Always involved in all sorts of civic projects." Connie's voice held a touch of affectionate apology. She loved her mother but, like a lot of people, had trouble liking her at times. Anna Jacobi had always blamed an unkind fate for her having been born on a ranch in Montana and not in a mansion in a city. She was happiest when she was running some committee or other and rubbing elbows with what she considered the right people. Vincent Martinelli, heir apparent to the Thurston Investments fortune, had, in Anna's opinion, been one of those people.

"She and Dad still live in Chicago. She really likes it there."

"Well, good. Good." Elsie nodded enthusiastically and smiled the way people do when they are unable to come up with a fitting response. She bustled back behind the counter and straightened a stack of yellowing brochures. "Land sakes, and here you are. Married? Any little ones?"

"No to both questions. I'm divorced." Pretending casualness, Connie wandered over to the sofa and chair set about a low, dusty table.

"Did my grandmother make these doilies?" she asked, her fingers smoothing one of the yellowing crocheted ovals that covered the armrests. "They remind me of the ones she used to have scattered about the house."

She hoped the subject of her marital status would be dropped. Kind people like Elsie invariably assumed that she was devastated by the divorce, and she wasn't. After two years of separation it had merely been the final severing of ties that had long ago ceased to bind in anything but name. Still, people felt the need to probe, perhaps to offer comfort. Connie welcomed neither, since she couldn't very well just come out and tell them that her ex-husband was an incurable philanderer and moreover had managed to keep her fooled for years.

No, she couldn't say that. Connie touched the doily gently. "Grandma always did such lovely needlework."

"Yes, she did, God rest her soul." Elsie lifted pious eyes to the ceiling. "Wonderful people, your grandfolks. Salt of the earth, both of them. They are sorely missed."

She paused a moment, then asked, "So where're you headed?"

Connie laid the memory of her grandparents to rest. She moved back to the counter, picked up a dog-eared registration form and started to fill in the blanks.

"For the moment," she replied, "I'm going to stay right here in your lovely motel while I wait for word from Paul Miller—"

"Paul Miller from over to the ranger station?" Elsie sounded intrigued.

"That's the one. He's my boss, and he's going to let me know when it's okay to drive up to Butler's Peak." Connie signed the form and looked up with a grin. "I'm the forest-fire lookout there this summer. What do you think of that?"

"Well, I never." Elsie shook her head in apparent wonder at the never-ending surprises life held in store.

Connie laughed as she dug around in her purse for a credit card. "Neither did I, Elsie, until about four months ago. That's when I came to visit my friend Helen who just happens to be married to Paul Miller."

Elsie took the proffered plastic and inspected it carefully. "Don't get too many of these," she muttered, bending to rummage beneath the counter. "Got the machine for it around here somewheres."

She reappeared with the dusty contraption, wiping and blowing at the grime before inserting the card. "So, how come you know Helen?"

"Years ago I went to college with her," Connie explained, fascinated by Elsie's careful validation of her credit card.

"I didn't stay to get my degree, but we kept in touch. And when I found myself temporarily at loose ends after finally graduating from the university early this spring she asked me to visit her in Hamilton. I did, and one thing led to another. I had a free summer, waiting for replies to the résumés I'd sent out, and somehow Paul talked me into taking the fire lookout training course."

Connie accepted the card Elsie was silently holding out to her and put it away. "I did, I passed, and I got this job. It'll be perfect. Great fun. Three months of nothing but wonderful, relaxing solitude before I start teaching school."

"Humph." The corners of Elsie's mouth curved sharply downward. Disapproval cloaked her like a shroud. "And I bet you believe in Santa Claus, too. Foolishness," she muttered, and selected a key from a row of hooks near the antiquated switchboard. Coming around the counter, she headed for the door.

"'Pears to me, Jud hasn't got word you'll be one of the lookouts, else he'd have had something to say, for sure. Reckon Paul knows what he's doing, though."

With a shrug at Elsie's mutterings, Connie followed her innkeeper out to the porch. "I'm putting you in number 6," she was told, and that made her remember Rudy.

"Say, Elsie..." Connie hurried to catch up. "You don't object to dogs in the room, do you? I have this Doberman...."

"Rudy, if you're not going to help, I'd just as soon you sat in the wagon and kept out of the way," Connie said as she tripped yet again over her loyal companion. "Your bags of food far outnumber my stuff, you know."

Rudy tended toward sloth. He chose to jump in the Bronco. Looking every inch the regal supervisor, he sat in the passenger seat and watched as Connie staggered by with a box full of books and loaded them in the back. He seemed to know that word had come from the ranger station; they were about to be on their way.

Paul Miller himself was going to guide them up to Butler's Peak.

"You stay while I run into the office and say goodbye to Elsie," Connie told Rudy after the last box was in place. "If Paul comes, tell him I'll be right out."

Rudy lay down and closed his eyes, as if he were exhausted from watching Connie work.

In the office, Elsie was not alone but deep in conversation with the man named Jud. He was dressed much the same as he had been the other day, and, Connie noted as he turned around, he was just as good-looking.

"Hi," she called out brightly to them both, walking up to stand next to Jud at the counter, careful not to get too close. Four days of not seeing him had not dimmed Connie's memory of the powerful effect his proximity and his gaze had had on her traitorous senses. She was determined to be merely polite, to say her goodbyes as quickly as possible and get herself out of there. "How's the vacation going?"

To her surprise, her neighborly inquiry was met with silence and a thorough inspection of her person by those clear greenish eyes of his. Eyes that, Connie noted, held no warmth today, only icy rejection.

Connie bristled, at a loss as to what she could have done to suddenly merit such obvious disapproval. Then she dismissed the question. Why should she care? After all, she need never speak with the man again.

She returned the stare with one of her own, deciding that he wasn't nearly as handsome as she'd thought. Without his hat, which lay on the counter in front of him, she could see that his dark head of hair was liberally sprinkled with gray. He looked old, she thought untruthfully, and he should have had a haircut weeks ago. And that tanned face of his could have done with a shave—again. Tempted to make some scathing comment, she decided instead to ignore him.

"Elsie," she said sweetly, turning to present her back to Jud whatever-his-name-was. "I'm all packed and ready. We'll be on our way as soon as Paul gets here. I can't tell you how much—"

The well-remembered deep voice interrupted her. "*I'll* be escorting you up the mountain, Mrs. Martinelli."

Connie drew herself up, briefly wishing she was taller. She faced him, the frost in her eyes matching his. "Pardon?"

"Connie, this here is Judson Halverson. He's—"

"The guy who's taking you up to the lookout." This time it was Elsie who was cut short. "Miller's busy. Now, if you're sure you mean to go through with this harebrained scheme, let's get it over with.''

Slamming the hat down on his head, Judson Halverson stalked over to the door. He looked about as anxious to guide her as he would be to catch Rocky Mountain spotted fever, Connie thought with extreme annoyance. And what did he mean, ''harebrained scheme''?

''If you've got more important things to do, Mr. Halverson,'' she informed him in tones that she hoped left little doubt that she thought it highly unlikely, ''please don't let me keep you. I assure you, I'm quite capable of driving myself up to Butler's Peak. I do have some maps, and—''

''Mrs. Martinelli—'' Halverson sounded put-upon ''—let's not get into a discussion of your capabilities at this time. I'm trying to be fair and reserve judgment. Now...'' He pulled open the door and made a sweeping motion with his arm. ''Shall we?''

Connie considered herself a reasonable human being, slow to anger, willing to get along with her fellows. Except this one. Follow him up the mountain? She'd rather walk blindfolded against traffic on Fifth Avenue. ''No,'' she declared, ''we shall not.''

Turning, she addressed Elsie, who looked bewildered. ''May I use your phone a moment?'' Then she added, ''Thank you,'' in response to the expected nod. The quick jerking motion of her finger as she dialed Paul Miller's number was the only indication of her inner turmoil.

She faced Halverson. He was leaning against the doorjamb, his arms crossed, looking bored. ''Hi, Paul, it's Connie,'' she said as soon as the Bitterroot Forest District's fire management officer came on the line. Keeping her eyes locked on the man in front of her, she rushed on. ''Listen, I— Yes, I'm ready, that's why I'm— What? Yes, he's here, but— *What?*''

Connie's eyes widened in disbelief at what she was hearing. Halverson was the picture of innocent unconcern, studying the nails of his left hand as though seeing them for the first time. When Connie squealed, *"The District Ranger?"* he intercepted her agonized gaze and, grinning, offered a helpless shrug of the what-can-I-say variety.

Inhaling deeply, Connie managed a dignified "Goodbye, Paul" and cradled the phone. Saying, "Thank you, Elsie," and "Ready when you are, Mr. Halverson," she swept out the door.

Connie was still fuming an hour later as she followed Halverson's pickup. She was nearly choking on the dust he stirred up, but she didn't dare fall too far behind on this narrow, winding mountain road. Clutching the wheel, she brooded over the fact that nobody had bothered to tell her that the "R.J." in front of "Halverson, District Ranger" stood for Raymond Judson—Jud, for short. Not that it had ever occurred to her to ask.

"He's the big cheese, Rudy," she glumly informed the dog. Rudy laid a consoling paw on her shoulder and growled.

Connie heaved a sigh. "You're right, I suppose. I shouldn't worry about it anymore. After all," she added with renewed indignation, "if the man had any *real* manners, he would have introduced himself right away instead of pulling all this cloak-and-dagger melodrama. Jerk," she added in a forceful mutter, slapping the palm of her hand on the steering wheel. The Bronco veered sharply to the left, and Connie hurried to apply her hand to the wheel again. How much farther did they have to go? she wondered, squinting through the windshield and hoping to see the end of the road.

Jud was whistling tonelessly as he drove, deep in thought. From time to time he checked the rearview mirror to see if his charge was still there. Yup, there she was, he noted, following his pickup with all the tenacity of a bloodhound on a scent. In somebody else he might have admired such spunk, but with Constance Martinelli he would have bet his hat it was nothing but sheer bravado. The woman was—a *woman*, dammit. The citified and pampered kind. In designer jeans and without a clue as to what she was up against.

He sighed. He could still hear Paul arguing that lots of women had been fire lookouts over the years. It was true. And Jud would have been the first to admit that almost without exception they were damn good at the job. But those women were locals, or at least they were accustomed to outdoor life. They were skilled with guns and fishing poles. This one didn't look as though she could wield anything more threatening than a damn nail file, for crying out loud.

Not that the lookout staffers had to live off the land, or anything like that. They hunted and fished for sport, like he did. And her training scores *had* been impressive, which meant that she knew and understood the equipment.... Oh, hell. Why didn't he quit kidding himself and admit he just plain didn't trust her? And why should he?

A twenty-eight-year-old *divorced*—that said something about her sense of responsibility right there—city woman. Obviously used to life in the fast lane. According to Elsie, the mother had always considered herself too good for the folks around here and had married some fancy society doctor in Chicago.

With that kind of background, how long would Constance Martinelli last all alone on a mountaintop, hundreds of miles from the nearest beauty parlor? What was to keep her, three days or three weeks from now, when the novelty of roughing it had worn off, from abandoning the lookout and leaving them high and dry and flammable?

On the other hand, Paul Miller seemed to trust her, and he'd been an excellent FMO nearly as long as Jud had been the district ranger. Which didn't mean he couldn't have let those big fawn eyes of Mrs. Constance Martinelli's cloud his judgment, of course. Even if she was Helen's friend.

Constance. Jud rolled the name around in his mind and navigated his truck around a piece of fallen rock. Such a big name for such a bitty thing. Connie suited her much better. Sounded kind of perky, like she herself tended to. She sure was cute when she got all huffy....

Irritated by the direction his thoughts were taking, Jud glared into the rearview mirror again. Sure enough, she was still there, enveloped in a cloud of dust.

Jud chuckled in spite of his irritation as he remembered her marching out the door in that silky pink blouse and those starchy blue jeans. What with the heat and the dust, she wasn't going to look quite so crisp by the time they got to where they were going.

Another glance in the rearview mirror had him laughing out loud. Oh, Lord, he wished he had a camera and could get a picture of that face. She looked mesmerized—nose to the windshield, eyes like saucers. He could all but feel the death grip she probably had on the wheel. He would have bet his new corral fence that this mountain road had her shaking in her fancy sneakers. Even that mutt of hers, sitting proud as you please in the passenger seat, looked a mite peaked.

Jud reminded himself that he'd best keep his own eyes front and center, too. The road up to the peak was a challenge even to a seasoned back-roads driver like himself. Carefully negotiating yet another hairpin curve, he was rewarded by a vista so spectacular that it never failed to take his breath away. Possessively, the way a lover eyes his beloved, he scanned the seemingly endless miles of forested mountains. This was his world, his home. He wondered if people like Connie, city people, knew how much they were missing, stuck in their asphalt jungles.

Of course, little Mrs. Martinelli was about to get a pretty good idea.

One more big curve and they'd be at the turnaround. Seeing it up ahead, Jud shifted down and slowed almost to a crawl. Connie's Bronco was practically attached to his bumper by now, he noted, but even so she kept right on going straight when he pulled off the road.

And then, when it apparently sunk in that he wasn't in front of her anymore, wouldn't you know she'd slam on the brakes and stall the damn engine again?

Jud shook his head in disbelief. Let's see, that made it three times this trip, near as he could figure. Twice before they'd gotten out of Slater's parking lot, for crying out loud. Why hadn't she just bought an automatic?

Stepping out of his truck, Jud watched as she glared at the dog, started the engine and maneuvered the wagon off the road ahead of the pickup. One look at her face and he had trouble keeping his straight. Best not to kid her about stalling right then, he decided.

He walked over and leaned in the window of the Bronco. A subtly floral fragrance, like alpine meadows in bloom, filled his nostrils. Her scent. He had noticed it the other day, when he'd opened the door for her at Elsie's. It had stirred something in him then, a fleeting desire to nuzzle those silky, wispy hairs at the back of her neck.

Now, mixed with the earth smell of dusty heat, its effect on him was much more powerful. Jud stepped back from the window.

"Are you just going to sit there?" The impatience in his tone was directed at himself more than at Connie.

Heaving a sigh that did disturbing things to the front of her blouse, she turned her head to look at him. "Are we there?"

"Just about."

"In that case, Rudy and I would just as soon keep going, and stretch our legs when we get there."

This time he did lose the battle against laughter. Damn, but she reminded him of that fancy bantam hen his mother had been so partial to. There'd been enough regal feistiness in that little body to intimidate the entire barnyard. A person had to constantly show her who was boss or be sorry.

Fighting to control his mirth, Jud removed his hat and studied it a moment before trusting himself to look into those wide hazel eyes of hers again. "I see Paul didn't tell you."

Her tawny, delicately shaped eyebrows rose, apparently in tandem with her temper. Her pale cheeks turned pink with annoyance beneath the film of dust. "Tell me what?"

"That it isn't possible to *drive* all the way up to Butler's Peak, Mrs. Martinelli. From here on up, we hoof it."

Two

Connie was furious with herself. How could she have forgotten that Butler's Peak was a walk-in fire lookout station? Paul had made quite a point of telling her, and she had been delighted, because it had made the place seem all the more private and peaceful.

Her hands tightened on the steering wheel they were still gripping after that harrowing drive. One look at the smirking ranger and Connie knew that as sure as this was Saturday he expected some kind of dismayed reaction from her. Well, she thought, he wasn't going to get it.

Struggling to unclench teeth and hands, Connie extracted the key from the ignition and jammed it in the pocket of her jeans. With her other hand she pulled at the door handle, and with a shove of her shoulder against the door she forcefully pushed it open. It slammed into Judson Halverson's midsection with a satisfying thud.

"Come on, Rudy, let's *hoof*," she said to the dog, pretending not to hear the ranger's choked oath or to see his look of almost comical surprise as he stood holding the door.

Rudy vaulted across Connie's lap and out of the wagon, leaving Connie to follow or not. She stepped past Raymond Judson Halverson, then stopped to look around. The scenery was breathtaking, the air crisp and fragrant with the scent of pine trees and alpine flora. Connie's heart swelled at the beauty of it, and hanging on to her irritation with the ranger became nearly impossible.

She snuck a peek at him to see if a conciliatory gesture might be welcome. He had closed the door of the Bronco and was watching her with his feet planted wide and his arms stiff at his sides. She couldn't decipher his expression, but it didn't look friendly.

Fine. Connie gave a mental shrug and crossed the road to the trail she had spotted there. It meandered upward through a rock-strewn meadow. With the intention of proving to the man how well she was able to cope and take charge, she started up the path.

She had climbed a fair piece before it sunk in that neither man nor beast seemed to be following. She stopped and looked back.

Halverson and the dog were watching her ascent. The district ranger was leaning against her wagon, arms folded across his broad chest and, judging by the white slash that split his tanned face, grinning. Rudy sat at attention at his feet, and she could have sworn he was grinning, too.

"Are you guys coming?" Connie called, one hand shading her eyes, the other planted on a hip. She didn't bother to conceal her impatient displeasure.

"No."

No? Connie glared down at the pair by the car from beneath her hand. It shook slightly as her temper went from simmer to boil. What did he mean, no? Did he intend to let her find her way up to the lookout alone? The way he was standing there, it sure looked like it. Well, *fine*. That was just dandy with her.

"In that case, I'll say goodbye, Mr. Halverson," she called, both hands now cupping her mouth. "Rudy, *come*."

Rudy obeyed, though with obvious reluctance. Connie added alienation of her dog's affections to the growing list of grievances against District Ranger Halverson. She turned her back on the both of them and marched on.

"Mrs. Martinelli!"

Now what? Connie turned to face downhill once again while Rudy's stub of a tail went into overdrive at the sound of Halverson's voice. Dumb mutt, Connie thought, fuming. It was bad enough *she* couldn't work up a genuine dislike for the man, but did Rudy have to fall for him like Macy's final clearance prices?

The ranger was beckoning with a gloved hand, still grinning. "You're going the wrong way." He pointed to a spot behind the pickup, laughing. "The trail to the lookout starts over here."

"Wh—" Connie's mouth dropped open, then snapped shut. Of all his childish stunts, this one won the prize. To think that the man had stood there and calmy watched her hike all this way up the wrong trail. Whyever had she thought he was a gentleman? Sadist seemed a much more fitting description right now.

He was waving an arm, yelling, "Did you hear me, Mrs. Martinelli?" He walked to the trail he had been pointing to. "This way."

Connie stayed where she was, watching with narrowed eyes as he headed up the hill. She thought of the way he had acted the first time they'd met, respectful and charming. Not at all like the wisecracking men she was used to from New York. Jud had been courteous, even kind, and she had been captivated.

But not today. Today he acted as if he had never seen her before. The looks he gave her alternated between amusement and disdain, and when he talked at all he either snapped or condescended. Connie neither liked nor understood any of it, and she had had enough.

Grimly she retraced her steps. Rudy was a black streak as he shot past her. Anger was a good fuel. Connie ran, too.

Halverson had not waited, and he didn't shorten his long strides as he hiked steadily upward. When at last she came abreast of him, Connie's breathing was labored.

"You could have told me I was going the wrong way." She hop-skipped a couple of steps, struggling to stay at his side.

"I did." Jud kept walking, not sparing her a glance.

"I mean sooner, dammit. I was halfway up the other side of the mountain." Another hop-skip. Why couldn't she have been born with long runner's legs?

Jud cocked a shaggy brow and shot her a sharp glance. It left Connie with little doubt about his opinion of her. "You were so busy communing with nature, I hated to interrupt."

Sarcasm. Connie disliked sarcasm. People resorted to it when they didn't have the guts to come right out and say what was really on their minds. She grabbed his sleeve and dug in her heels, forcing him to stop. They were going to have this out, by God, right here and right now.

"You don't like me, do you?" she charged, shaking his arm. "I want to know why."

Halverson, looking pained, picked her fingers off his sleeve and turned to walk on.

"Oh, no, you don't." In a flash Connie darted ahead of him and blocked his path. Even though she stood on slightly higher ground, she still had to lean her head back in order to glare into his face.

"We're staying right here," she announced, placing a restraining hand against his chest, "until I get an answer."

Jud pursed his lips. He seemed to be considering the question. He looked pointedly at the hand on his chest.

Connie hastened to remove it but otherwise stayed where she was. She would not be intimidated.

The eyes that met hers looked as cold as ice. Jud stuck both hands in the back pockets of his jeans and shifted his weight to one foot. Connie's throat closed, and she shivered, wishing she could pull her gaze away from the frostiness of his but determined not to back off.

Halverson's brows lowered as he stared at her, betraying the impatient annoyance he obviously felt. "I neither like nor dislike you, Mrs. Martinelli," he said coldly. "I don't know you. What I do know is that you're wrong for the job and don't belong here."

"How can you say that?" Connie demanded, stung by his out-of-hand rejection of her. "I finished the training course at the top of the class!"

"Learning and doing are two different things, Mrs. Martinelli. Theoretical knowledge alone doesn't prepare you for the realities of living and working at a fire lookout station. Out here there is no handy instructor around to correct mistakes—some of which can have very serious consequences."

Halverson abandoned his casual stance and leaned closer. He stabbed an accusing finger into the air near Connie's shoulder.

"Tell me, Mrs. Martinelli, what does someone like you know about living all alone on top of a mountain, or anywhere, for that matter? I only have to look at your fancy duds and your soft little hands to know you don't have the slightest idea about what you're up against with this job. Hell..."

With patent exasperation Jud spun on his heel and continued his climb, leaving Connie to stare at his back.

She was mad. "I can handle this job every bit as well as the next guy, Ranger Halverson," she called after him, earning herself a glare over a rigidly set shoulder.

She hurried to catch up with him. "You don't know anything about me at all," she said accusingly.

"Enough to know I'd never have hired you," the ranger replied. Then he added, "But you're Paul Miller's responsibility, not mine."

"Then why don't you just let *him* worry about my incompetence and cool your jets," Connie snapped, her ego severely dented by Halverson's assessment and cool dismissal of her qualifications.

"I intend to."

"Fine."

They tramped on in silence, Rudy at their heels. Connie was fuming, and more than a little hurt. She was outgoing and friendly, and she had been prepared to like Judson Halverson, had thought him attractive. It stung to realize that he was not the least bit similarly inclined.

At last, after they rounded yet another bend, the lookout building came into view. They stopped, and Connie gulped for air. Jud's breathing was as even as ever.

"Well, there it is," he said, pointing to the building but looking at her. "Home."

Connie forced her features into a display of delighted interest. "Great," she exclaimed, walking closer.

The structure consisted of two boxlike stories. The lower box had a couple of tiny windows. The upper one, topped by a gabled roof, appeared to have no windows at all. A porch encircled the second story, and Connie stopped at the foot of the stairs leading up to it. From where she stood, she could see that the upstairs windows were shuttered.

"Very nice," Connie said, hands in pockets and tongue in cheek. If she had hated it, she still would have said it was nice rather than give him any kind of opening for criticism. She offered an enthusiastic smile.

The ranger climbed the stairs without comment, but his quirked brow made it plain that he was not fooled by her sudden cheerfulness.

Rudy had circled the building, nose to the ground. He seemed satisfied that all was well and ran off to explore farther afield. About to call him back, thinking he might get lost, Connie changed her mind. She followed the ranger upstairs, telling herself that if Rudy was going to live here he had to check things out just as she did.

Jud stood on the porch and scraped a gloved finger along the handrail, loosing weathered brownish flakes. "This whole place needs painting," he observed over his shoulder. "That can be your first job when you're settled in. Paint and tools should be down in the storage room. If they aren't, order them."

Connie frowned at his back. "I thought my job was to spot and report fires."

"It is," Jud drawled. When he half turned and shot her that hateful, amused look again, Connie wished she'd just kept her mouth shut. After all, she'd known that maintenance of the lookout facility would be part of the job—in theory. She had imagined maintenance to mean keeping clean rather than restoring.

"Keeping the lookout from falling apart is also part of your job, as I'm sure you were told," the ranger went on. "Believe me, without those extra chores you'd get mighty bored."

Connie doubted it. She had brought plenty of books, and she also had a life to plan. But this time she kept her own counsel. She walked along the porch away from him, moodily conducting an inspection of her own.

"Mrs. Martinelli, help me get these shutters off, will you?" Jud was around a corner, rattling and pounding some uncooperative boards.

Connie pushed herself away from the railing she had been leaning on and went to lend a hand. "Mrs. Martinelli," she muttered sourly. "I wish he'd drop the phony formality."

She reached up to hold the panel in place so that Jud could use both hands to loosen the bar that lay across it.

Searching his face out of the corner of her eyes, Connie belatedly wondered if he had heard her muttered complaint. She hoped not.

Jud's face revealed nothing. With silent efficiency he dispensed with the bar, laid it on the porch and pulled the shutter panel out. He leaned it against the rail and turned to the next window. Together, not speaking, they quickly took down one shutter after another.

The last window bared, they reached the door. Jud took out a set of keys, fitted one in the lock and turned it. Pushing the door open with one hand, he stood aside and handed the keys to Connie with the other. "These are yours, *Connie*," he said. "Don't lose them."

So he *had* heard. The way he'd stressed her name made Connie's temper rise. "Why, thank you, *Raymond*," she replied with equal mockery, dropping the keys down the front of her shirt. "I'll guard them with my life."

With that she had intended to sweep past him into the combination living room and workroom. His hand stopped her. It encircled Connie's upper arm like a vise and held her immobile in front of him in the open doorway. Their gazes locked.

"Nobody calls me Raymond." Jud's voice was low, a fierce whisper, and he enunciated each word carefully. It seemed an eternity before his hold on her arm eased and became gentle, and all the while they stared at each other as if hypnotized.

Connie felt trapped by the compelling brightness of Judson Halverson's eyes, much like a rabbit caught in the headlights of an oncoming car. Heart pounding, she watched as, little by little, the brilliance of his anger dimmed and fires of another sort ignited.

When his gaze released hers and shifted to her lips, Connie's breath caught. He lowered his head with unmistakable intent, and still she could not move except to rise on tiptoe to meet him.

Breathlessly Connie awaited the kiss she hadn't known she'd been craving until that very moment. Her eyelids drifted shut, and she savored the heat of Jud's breath on her parted lips. Now, she thought. And then . . . nothing.

Connie's eyes flew open and stared into his. They were no longer bright, but opaque, guarded. His face, no longer close, was equally inscrutable. "Are you all right?" he asked, his voice almost a growl.

Connie wrenched her gaze from his and fought to bring order into her rattled brain. Her fingers were still curled in Jud's shirtfront, clutching it. Her thoughts raced. He hadn't intended to kiss her at all. How could she have thought he had and made such a fool of herself?

"I'm fine," she said through lips that felt stiff and cold but were stretched in a smile nonetheless. She concentrated on releasing and smoothing his shirt. Beneath her hand his heartbeat was strong and fast. Very fast.

Connie lifted her eyes back to Jud's and, catching him unawares, found the flames there not quite extinguished after all. Yet, his brow was creased and his expression was troubled.

Connie's embarrassment fled with the realization that while Judson Halverson might not approve of Constance Martinelli the lookout staffer he was not indifferent to Connie the woman. Filing the knowledge away for future consideration, she vowed to change his professional opinion of her, starting right now.

"So," she said, stepping away from him and farther into the room, "these are my quarters." She looked around with genuine interest.

Right before her, on a high table in the center of the room, was the azimuth, the instrument whose function it was to pinpoint the precise geographical location of a fire. It was the focal point of the bright, sparsely furnished second story. A narrow bed, a few shelves, a table and two chairs were all painted white, and were strictly utilitarian. A small stove and an even smaller refrigerator occupied a corner.

"All the comforts of home," Jud commented from his position by the door. He sounded like himself again.

Ignoring the steady regard that she felt rather than saw, Connie made no reply as she moved around the room. The two-way radio, her link to civilization, sat on a shelf below the azimuth. Crouching down in front of it, she looked it over. It was identical to the one they had used in class. She reached out a hand to flip the on-off switch to on, selected channel 1, which was used for general forestry business, and got up. There, she thought, stifling the urge to thumb her nose at Jud and his doubts. Butler's Peak was now officially operational. She continued her tour.

A large, chipped enamel bowl next to a dry and cracked bar of soap on a saucer graced the top of a small cupboard. Two towel racks stuck out like sagging antennae from the side of it, and two large buckets sat on the floor below.

Except for the door, every wall was made transparent by the windows facing in all directions. Through one of them, some twenty feet down a well-trodden trail, Connie spotted a small building discreetly sheltered by a stand of stunted pines. Ah, yes ... Her eyebrows rose as she recognized its function. All the comforts of home.

She turned to look across the room at Jud, a flippant remark on her lips. She swallowed it unsaid. He was studying her intently, looking sober and thoughtful but otherwise relaxed. He leaned against the doorjamb, arms and feet crossed, in what Connie was beginning to think of as his favorite pose.

Their gazes tangled. Connie's heart skipped a beat before lodging in her throat and making her breathless again. For long moments the kiss that hadn't happened seemed to hang between them like an unsung melody.

Oh, no, Connie thought resolutely, not again. Forcing her eyes away from him, she marched to the door. Time to get rid of the district ranger. She all but bolted down the stairs and over to the trail.

First Rudy, back from his explorations, and then Jud caught up with her. "Don't you want me to show you the rest of it?" Jud asked. Whatever he had been brooding about back at the lookout had apparently been resolved. He seemed to be in excellent humor. "What about the storage room? Or the outhouse?"

Connie was sure he was trying to solicit some appalled reply about the latter. "No, thank you. I'll see the storage room when I store some of my things, and I saw the outhouse from the window."

"Not the inside."

She shot him a saucy look. "I'll just look forward to touring it later. Alone."

"Never know what's nesting in there after the long winter."

That almost got to Connie, but right then her need to see Judson Halverson gone was greater than her fear of crawly creatures. Besides, she reasoned, witnessing her squeamish reaction would only reinforce his already uncomplimentary opinion of her as a hopeless tenderfoot.

She stepped up her pace, and they arrived at the turnaround and stopped next to Connie's car in what seemed like no time at all.

She turned to face him. "Mr. Halverson, we—"

"Jud," the ranger said, a crooked grin creasing his features in an almost endearing way. "No phony formality, remember?"

Connie did remember, all of it. Still, she managed a gracious smile and inclined her head. "Jud. As I was about to say, Rudy and I are grateful to you for guiding us up here, but we'll be fine now. There's really no need for you to stay any longer."

She pulled her car keys out of her pocket and busied herself unlocking the rear gate of the wagon.

"You don't want my help unloading?" Jud removed his hat, scratching his head and resettling the Stetson in one practiced motion. Hooking his thumbs into his belt, he rocked back on his heels and peered at Connie from beneath the brim of his hat.

"No, thank you," Connie said with what she hoped was firm finality. "You've done much more than you would ordinarily, I'm sure." She pulled the nearest box closer and lifted it.

"No more than your FMO would have done if he hadn't been called out of town," Jud replied curtly, snatching the box out of her hands and setting it on the ground between them.

"No! I don't need—"

"Save your breath." He took hold of an arm and propelled her away. "I'm only going to show you your spring before I leave."

They trooped over to a piece of hose protruding from an embankment. "This is it right here." Jud released Connie's arm as ungraciously as he had grasped it and bent to pick up the hose to demonstrate the gentle flow. Straightening, he lifted it to his mouth and drank.

Connie rubbed at the spot where Jud had gripped her and watched the bobbing Adam's apple in the strong, tanned column of his throat. Heaven help her, she found his drinking sexy. Boy, were her hormones making up for lost time! As Jud quenched his thirst, her own lips became parched. She felt compelled to wet them with her tongue.

"Here." Jud extended the hose toward Connie. Her gaze shifted to it and back up to his face. He was wiping his mouth with the back of his hand. His eyes gleamed. Connie was sure he had guessed her thoughts, but all he said was "Have some. It's cold and pure."

Connie hesitated before gingerly accepting the hose from Jud. Though it was awkward, and an admittedly childish gesture, she tried not to put her mouth to the spot Jud had drunk from. There, she thought, that should wipe the smug grin from his face.

It didn't. It made him chuckle. She ignored the deep rumble of it and sipped at the hose, in the process splashing more of the cool liquid *on*to than *in*to herself. It didn't matter. After all the dust the water felt and tasted wonderful.

"Better than the stuff in the city, you've got to admit," Jud offered.

"If you say so." Connie dropped the hose and stifled the urge to remind him that at least in the city the stuff flowed from faucets inside houses and not from a hose a quarter mile down a mountain. "The thought will sustain me when I'm hauling buckets of it up to the lookout," she said, then smiled a quick apology for the sarcasm.

"Want me to fetch the first couple?" Jud asked.

"Oh, no." Connie's smile turned upside down. The man must really think she was totally helpless. "I will do it myself. Thank you."

Jud scowled, looked as if he might insist, then nodded. "Right."

They regarded each other in silence, and for a moment Connie could have sworn she detected something like grudging respect in the fathomless depths of his eyes. She called herself a dreamer.

"I'd better get busy," she said, but didn't move.

"Yeah," Jud replied. He removed his hat, studied it as if it were a foreign object, then slammed it back on his head. "I'll leave you to it, then."

He pivoted, strode over to the forest-service pickup and folded his tall frame into the seat. He revved the engine before executing a neat turn on the narrow turnaround. "Good luck," he called through the open window, touching a finger to the brim of his hat.

Nodding her thanks, Connie stood at the spring and watched the pickup disappear in a cloud of dust. Inexplicably, as soon as Jud was out of sight, she felt bereft. Abandoned. For just a moment in the sudden silence panic paralyzed her limbs. My God, she wondered with a touch of hysteria, what am I doing here all alone?

Something cold and damp bumped her hand. Jerking it away, she stared down into Rudy's shiny black eyes.

"Oh, Rudy." Weak with relief, Connie knelt and hugged the dog. She kissed his silky muzzle. "I'm not alone, am I?"

Rudy sat patiently while Connie drew strength from his closeness. She was fine, she told herself, just a little overwhelmed by the many new impressions.

She nuzzled the dog's neck and heaved a shaky sigh. New impressions, and District Ranger Halverson. Never before had she come up against anyone so contradictory. He changed his tune quicker and more often than a deejay changed records. And the disturbing thing was that, polite, folksy, charming, rude—no matter what—the man drew the most unsettling responses from her. He constantly put her on the defensive, yet back at the lookout she had wanted his kiss more than she had ever wanted anything before. She had trembled at his touch, had yearned for just a tiny taste of him.

And, remembering, she still did.

"Oh, Rudy." Connie pressed her flushed face against the Doberman's sleek coat. "This is all so crazy. Nothing's going the way I thought it would."

She drew back and framed his head with her hands, looking at him. "Maybe we ought to go back where we came from, boy. Hmm?"

She stroked his short, pointy ears. "Except you know what he'll say then? He'll say he knew all along we weren't cut out for the job. But we're going to show him, aren't we?"

Rudy stared back at her with dignity and affection but kept his thoughts to himself. When he stood, most of his hindquarters wagged. His tongue darted out and swiped at

Connie's face before he pulled out of her grip and backed away a few steps. He looked over at the wagon, then back at Connie, and gave a short, encouraging bark. "Come on," he seemed to be saying. "Let's go."

Back and forth they went, up and down the trail, until Connie could have pinpointed the location of every rock and pebble blindfolded. Sneakers, she came to realize, were not the ideal footwear for hiking on mountain trails all day long.

While Connie fetched and carried more supplies and belongings than she would ever have imagined she possessed, Rudy made like a hunter, darting hither and yon with his nose to the ground.

"Times like this I wish you were a husky," Connie muttered, panting, her final load balanced precariously on tired arms. "At least then I could have made you help with the hauling."

Obviously secure in the knowledge that Doberman pinschers were not pack animals, Rudy ran up the steps with undiminished energy.

Connie trudged along in his wake. "I swear, these have gotten steeper," she groaned. "Rudy, why didn't you stop me when I told the ranger I didn't want his help?"

Inside the room, she carefully picked her way through the obstacle course of her belongings on the floor and deposited her load on top of a small cupboard. Arching her aching back, she pressed both hands to the small of it. Every bone, every muscle, ached.

A hot shower, Connie thought longingly. Slowly turning, she looked at the washstand and the chipped enamel bowl. All right, a warm sponge bath. Followed by a long soak of her feet. Her eyes dropped lower, coming to rest on the two buckets beneath the stand. The two *empty* buckets. For quite a while she contemplated them, and then she sighed.

Dropping her hands, she turned to Rudy, who was still by the door. "No bath and no dinner tonight, my friend, 'cause I'm not going back down there again. I'm just too damn tired."

Since he'd already eaten his daily ration of dog food and hated baths with a passion, Rudy took the announcement like a trouper.

Connie made her way back to the door and peered at the sky. "It's getting dark," she said, going in search of a broom and some toilet tissue. "Time to inspect the outhouse."

Three

———

The first thing Connie heard when she awoke was silence. No, she decided, keeping her eyes shut, she heard Rudy's soft snores, but nothing else that was familiar. No cars, no people, no radios—none of the sounds that even, in tiny Mattville, had been part of waking up. The silence was eerie, and more than a little unsettling.

She had dreamed of Judson Halverson in the night, Connie remembered. He had kissed her, and that had been more than a little unsettling, too.

Please, she told her befogged brain, not now. Dealing with that irritating ranger all day, as well as through the night, had been plenty.

Connie wrenched open gritty eyes. They felt as if the sandman had accidentally dumped his entire load into them. Lifting her arms to rub away residual sleep, she flinched and groaned. God, she hurt. Everywhere.

Blinking at the brightness, she struggled to sit up amid the tangle of itchy wool blankets and twitching dog legs. One

look at the scattered stacks, boxes and bags of her belongings and she plopped right down again.

Chaos. Connie gave herself up to another groan, then
forced her aching limbs upright and eased herself off the
bed.

"Get up, sleeping beauty." Each movement a painful reminder of yesterday's travails, she bent to pull at the blanket, shaking Rudy's inert form. "Up, up, up."

Rudy opened one eye, yawned, stretched and closed it
again. Disgusted, Connie turned away, only to be confronted by a caricature of herself in the mirror above the
washstand.

Arrested by the gruesome sight, she stared, openmouthed and horrified. Smeared mascara, cheeks streaked
with a mixture of dust, blush and sweat. A sunburned nose.
My God, Connie thought, aghast, she looked like a rac-
coon that had been through the wringer. Literally.

Her hair! With trembling hands, Connie attempted to
finger-comb the tangled dusty-yellow mop. Unsuccessful,
she settled for a couple of pats in an effort to compress it,
then let her hands slide down her woebegone face.

Her hands! Connie's eyes widened and filled as she
watched those abused appendages drop from view. She
backed away from the mirror and held them up. Blistered,
filthy skin, chipped polish, and broken nails— Oh God!

Connie knew it was silly, but she had always been vain
about her hands. Now, seeing the wreckage, she choked on
a groan and buried her face in them.

Her growling stomach a dismal accompaniment, Connie
struggled against the urge to cry, to call it quits then and
there. And to run as fast as she could back to New York,
where she belonged.

Oh, yeah? some rebel voice inside her jeered. She dropped
her hands into her lap and stared down at them. But this
time what she saw was not blisters, dirt and broken nails but
crowded subways, smog and Vincent Martinelli. Did she

really want to go back to the place where Vincent could call her up and make her life miserable anytime he chose—as he had for a month before she'd finally been able to leave?

No, thanks. Connie slapped hands on knees and resolutely lifted her chin. No way. Besides—she surveyed her surroundings with a jaundiced eye—she had never been a quitter. Never. Even in her marriage she had hung in there and tried long after everyone else had told her to cut her losses and—

"Mattville ranger station calling Butler's Peak lookout. Over."

The unexpected voice shattered the mountaintop's silence and Connie's introspection like a thunderclap, causing her to jump clear off the bed. What on earth?

"Butler's Peak, do you read? Over."

That voice again. That man. Judson Halverson. What could he want, for Pete's sake, except to check up on her?

Connie bristled. Wouldn't you know it? she thought, directing the force of her ire toward the set. Halverson had left less than twenty-four hours ago and already he expected her to be in trouble. Hoped for it, she would bet. Just so he could say he'd known all along Martinelli couldn't hack it.

Well, to hell with you and your assumptions, Mr. High-and-Mighty Halverson, Connie fumed. *Martinelli damn well can hack it.*

She stalked over to the radio and snatched up the microphone. "This is Butler's Peak. I read you loud and clear, Ranger Halverson." In more ways than one, she added silently, proud that her voice sounded cool and competent, if a shade belligerent. As an afterthought she added the word "Over" to her transmission, then released the button so that she could hear his reply.

When she heard his maddening chuckle, she wished she hadn't bothered.

"Did I wake you, Butler's Peak? You sound a mite grouchy this morning, and on such a bright and sunny day, too. Is everything all right?"

Was it sunny? Connie hadn't stopped to notice. Stepping up to the window, she looked out.

The world ouside fairly shimmered beneath a cloudless sky, the pines and grasses stirring in the gentle breeze. She took a deep breath and propped her elbows on the cupboard that doubled as a windowsill. Her nose all but pressed to the glass, she drank in the sparkling scenery.

"Rudy and I have been up for hours," she informed the ranger, uttering the lie without any qualms whatsoever. After all, she told her protesting conscience, he was not calling just to be neighborly, or even in the line of duty. He was calling to spy on her. That made him practically an enemy, and nowhere was it written that you had to be truthful with your enemies.

"You know what they say," she added, grinning to herself. *"A quien madruga Dios le ayuda."*

"God helps those who get up early," Jud promptly replied in a perfect translation of the Spanish proverb her parents' Puerto Rican housekeeper had been so fond of quoting.

Connie's grin turned sour. Was there no catching the man at a disadvantage?

Pulling away from the window, Connie walked back to the radio shelf, strongly tempted to simply disconnect the call and stick her tongue out at the aggravating man at the other end.

"I didn't know you spoke Spanish," he was saying, "but that certainly is a good motto to follow. I take it you're all settled, then."

Connie grimaced. "You wouldn't know the place." Well she rationalized, looking around, that was true. It would take her till nightfall, at least, to make it look like anything Halverson would recognize.

"Any problems? Anything you need from here?"

A crew from Rent-A-Maid would be nice, Connie thought wistfully. And how about an exterminator for the outhouse? She shuddered, visions of last night's debacle rising before her. Armed with broom and flashlight, she had been swatting at huge, hairy spiders and their sticky webs, all the while expressing her revolted aversion with screeches and yelps that had had poor Rudy cowering among the shubbery.

Her first project of the day would be to scour the outhouse. Followed by a head-to-toe scrub of her person, in cold water if necessary, and—Connie flinched, pained by the thought—a ruthless stripping and trimming of her nails.

Having formulated a new plan of action, Connie was eager to get on with it. "There are no problems I can't handle, Ranger Halverson. As a matter of fact, in a day or two I should be well enough organized to have a better idea of what I am up against. I will draw up a detailed work schedule for the bigger projects, as well as a list of any supplies I'll be needing."

She paused a beat, then added, "I'm just a teensy bit confused about one thing, Jud." Her voice was pure treacle. "With you spending so much of your valuable time worrying about me and all, wouldn't it be simpler if I reported only to you, and to heck with the fire-management officer?"

Damn. Jud set his jaw and glared at the radio set. The woman was right. He had no legitimate reason for checking up on her, and he knew it. Trouble was, she knew it, too, and she couldn't resist letting him know it.

Well, sir, he thought, picking up the microphone one last time, enough of that.

"You'll report to the FMO, Mrs. Martinelli," he said, his tone matching her earlier professional briskness. "Over and out."

Replacing the mike, Jud flipped the switch and got out of Paul Miller's chair. He headed for his own office, thoroughly disgusted with himself. He had come in to the station today to look through the mail and get it sorted out in peace before officially returning to work tomorrow. The radio had seemed to beckon, to downright dare him to check up on the new lookout.

With a savage curse, Jud dropped into the chair behind the desk and cradled his head in his hands. He could sit here and tell himself he'd called Butler's Peak because its staffer was new and inexperienced and Paul Miller was out of the office, but that would be a lie.

Jud didn't like to lie, least of all to himself. He had called Connie Martinelli today for the same reason he'd sent Paul on some drummed-up errand yesterday—so he could check her out. So he could catch her messing up. So he could prove to Paul Miller that he'd made a mistake in hiring this glossy little baby doll.

Well—Jud lifted his head and rubbed his burning eyes—he had struck out on all counts. The woman obviously had plenty of gumption and was coping just fine. Paul's faith in her seemed to be justified, and he—Jud—had been wrong. End of story, right?

Wrong.

Restless, impatient with himself, Jud jumped to his feet and paced the office. Dammit, he still wasn't being honest. He was attracted to the woman, powerfully so.

Jud stopped by the window and rested a forearm against its wooden frame. His head hurt, and he dropped his furrowed brow against the cool glass. He didn't want to be attracted to Mrs. Constance Martinelli, couldn't even understand why he was. She was too short. Jud had always had an eye for long, shapely legs. She was pretty, but far less so than many others who had left him cold.

Jud lifted his head and stared up at the mountains as if the answer could somehow be found among their ancient rocks.

She was too young—twelve long years too young! From the city, spoiled and pampered. Divorced, by God.

Jud Halverson, descendant of German and Norwegian farmers, had had respect for law and order, marriage and motherhood beaten into him by a strict father. He did not believe in divorce, and that was one of the reasons he had never wanted to get married.

Well, almost never. Ten years ago there had been Ruth. She hadn't been from around these parts, but she'd lived in Hamilton for years and she'd fitted right in. She'd been special. Full of fun, yet practical, too.

Jud pulled himself up short. Ruth was dead. But he was alive, and until recently he hadn't been lonely as a bachelor. Time was when he hadn't been averse to casual sex when it was offered, and it had been offered often enough to keep him from getting ornery.

At least until he'd woken up one morning pushing forty and wondering if that was all there'd ever be for him. And he'd gotten to thinking that maybe it was time to settle down.

But how? And with whom? What was love, and where did a body find a steady and compatible woman to share forever?

Jud heaved a long sigh, the mountains he stared at a blur as he focused on the persistent mental image of Constance Martinelli. What she made him feel was not love, he reminded himself fiercely, but physical attraction, lust. Sexual appeal had a way of blinding people to the differences between them, usually with disastrous results.

He thought of Lars Erickson, boyhood friend and son of his family's closest neighbor. Lars had met a beautiful young woman while in the service and brought her back to the ranch. Less than a year later she had run off, leaving Lars with a broken heart and an infant child.

It wasn't a fate Jud cared to share.

* * *

"Helen's been telling me all along that your marinara sauce is the best there is, but until I tasted it myself yesterday I never believed it."

On his way out of the office, Jud caught the tail end of what sounded as if it might have been a lengthy discourse on a certain party's spaghetti sauce. He knew immediately which lookout his FMO was talking to.

Jud was late for a meeting, but he stopped to listen to the rest of the conversation anyway. This was the first time he had happened to be around when Connie was checking in, and he might as well find out how she had survived her first ten days on the job. He'd been too busy to think of her—well, a good part of the time, anyway.

"I'm glad you liked it, Paul." Connie's voice came over the radio clear as a bell. She sounded so cheerful that Jud found it irksome. It sure seemed like she was having one helluva good time up on that mountain. Had she done the painting?

"Helen insisted on taking the leftovers from our lunch home to you," she was saying now. "Did she tell you we wallpapered the outhouse?"

Jud winced. *What?*

Paul chuckled. "Yeah, she did. I saw the paper she bought for it, too. Black on white—stock-market listings, wasn't it?"

"That's the one. I thought it might add a touch of class. Say..." Connie suddenly sounded almost breathless with excitement. "I've got to go. Company's coming. Tourists, by the look of them, and I'm standing here practically naked. Talk to you tomorrow, Paul. Over and out."

As Paul laughed and flipped the switch, Jud struggled to dispel the vision of a scantily clad blonde, as well as the urge to hightail it up to the lookout and order those tourists off the property.

He released the doorknob and walked over to the FMO desk in the corner. "Was that Butler's Peak?"

Leaning a hip against Paul's desk, hands stuffed into the pockets of his uniform pants, he hoped his casual stance would convey nothing but idle curiosity. "How is...uh, Martinelli, wasn't it? How is Martinelli working out up there?"

Paul tilted his chair back and folded his hands behind his head. He grinned up at Jud. "She's doing great, Jud. Really fine. Helen was up to see her yesterday—"

"So I heard just now. Busy social life—"

"Says Connie's got the place looking pretty good."

"Yeah, wallpaper in the outhouse—"

"Paid for with her own money, boss."

Jud frowned. "What about the lookout building? Has she found time to paint that, with all the fancy redecorating she's doing?"

When he saw Paul's smile thin and his eyebrows rise, Jud wished he had moderated his tone. Dammit to hell, why was it that just talking about the woman raised his blood pressure?

"Well?" he growled when Paul just lay back and eyed him with a peculiar look on his face.

Paul dropped his arms and slowly righted his chair. "She's about half-done," he said mildly, "which is right on with the other lookouts. I'm telling you, boss, she's doing great."

"We'll see about that when we get a hot spell and some fires."

Paul shot him another strange look from beneath arched brows, and Jud wished he'd learn to remember that the woman was Paul's responsibility, not his.

He pushed away from the desk and walked away.

Paul's voice followed him. "Helen's been asking after you, Jud. Why don't you come for supper Saturday night?"

Already halfway out the door, Jud stopped. Helen was an excellent cook, and he always had a good time with the

Millers. He turned toward Paul, who was busy shuffling papers.

"I'm taking Kris Morgan out to a movie that night. I don't suppose I can bring her along?"

At that, Paul swiveled around in his chair, frowning. "You dating Kris now?"

Jud shrugged, thinking that the eligible women around here were no more fun now than they had ever been. None of them had any surprises in store for him. They were nice, steady, dependable . . . dull. "We've gone out a time or two. Nothing serious."

Paul nodded thoughtfully. "Nice woman, Kris. But, you know, I think Helen hardly knows her. She probably wouldn't be all that comfortable if you brought Kris to the house. How about you alone meeting us for Sunday brunch at the Golden Spur instead?"

"Well, all right." Jud had never known Helen Miller to be uncomfortable in any social situation he could think of, but he was willing to concede the issue to Paul. "Won't be the same as eating Helen's home cooking, but I'll be there and glad of the company."

"Great." Paul beamed. "Make it eleven-thirty."

The clock above the cash register read 11:45 when Marty, longtime hostess at the popular Golden Spur, instructed Jud to please follow her to the Miller table. Marty, almost as tall as Jud and half again as wide, obscured his forward view as they made their stately way into and through the large, crowded dining room. Jud clutched his gray Sunday Stetson in both hands and looked left and right instead.

Most of the men were dressed as he was—Western-cut suit, pastel-colored Western-style shirt and string tie. In Jud's case the suit was gray, the shirt pink, the tie maroon. Some of the women were giving him frankly admiring glances that Jud reciprocated with pleasure.

The mellow strains of some piped-in music competed valiantly with the din created by dozens of conversations, bursts of laughter and the clink and clatter of dishes and silverware. The air was heavy with the mixture of odors in which strong coffee and fried bacon predominated.

Marty had come to a stop, and Jud, winking at a particularly friendly-looking young woman, bumped into the hostess's back. Taking a quick step backward, he reached out a steadying hand. "Excuse me, Marty."

"Quite all right, Jud." Marty displayed a splendid set of dentures and stepped aside, indicating the table. "Here we are. Enjoy your meal, folks."

"Thanks." Jud watched her sail away, then turned to greet his friends. His smile froze.

Connie Martinelli was staring at him, her emotions obviously as mixed as his own. Surprise, resentment, pleasure...all quickly masked by a look of neutrality. Jud's pulse quickened, their differences forgotten. She looked wonderful, but somehow changed.

"Finally." Paul was on his feet and clapping Jud's shoulder. "You old son of a gun, I was beginning to wonder what had happened to you."

Jud tore his gaze away from Connie's and addressed his friend. "Damn car wouldn't start. Ended up taking the pickup."

"Well, now that you're here, don't just stand there, the two of you. Hi, Jud."

"Hi, gorgeous." Jud bent to kiss Helen's cheek. "Aren't you a sight for sore eyes?"

Helen blushed, her eyes sparkling. "Go on with you. Hurry up and sit over there next to Connie so we can have some champagne."

Jud excused himself as he squeezed past the adjacent table and folded his length into the chair across from Helen. For a moment he felt nearly as awkward as he'd felt in his

youth the one and only time he'd gone on a blind date. He
almost laughed aloud at his own foolishness.

"Good morning, Mrs.—uh, Constance." Without
meaning to, he bumped his knee into her thigh as he settled
himself more comfortably. He flashed her a smile. "Good
to see you again."

"Good morning." Connie's voice was cool. She no longer
seemed to be the least bit discomfited by his appearance.
Could he have misread her initial reaction to seeing him?

She moved her chair to allow more room for his legs.
Their shoulders touched. Each of them jerked back as if
jolted by a shock of electricity. Then, catching each other's
expressions, they exchanged identical looks of chagrin.

"Excuse me," Jud murmured.

"It's okay." Connie ventured a tentative smile.

Seeing that smile and her face, devoid of makeup, so close
he could see freckles sprinkled all over it like brown sugar
on a spice cake, Jud thought she looked good enough to eat.
He had to clear his throat twice before he could trust his
voice.

"I didn't know you'd be here."

"I didn't expect to see you, either," she replied, "or I
probably wouldn't have come."

Jud's pride was pricked. "Why not, for crying out loud?"

Connie tossed her head and looked down her nose at him.
"I prefer to spend my free time with friends, thank you."

"And I guess we're not. Friends, that is."

She laughed. "Hardly."

"Well, maybe we could be," Jud heard himself say. What
was worse, he knew he meant it. Something about this
woman made him want to throw common sense to the
winds, but he'd make darn sure things between them stayed
platonic.

He held out his hand. "How about it? Truce?"

Connie took her time placing the tips of her fingers in his
palm. "Okay," she finally said. "Since we're both friends

of Paul and Helen, I guess it would make things easier all around."

Paul and Helen...Jud had forgotten about them. He cast a quick look at the couple across the table. They were apparently deep in their own conversation, the picture of smugness, smiling benignly, the way people did when they'd just pulled a fast one on some unsuspecting sucker.

Jud looked away with an inward chuckle, thinking that those sly little rascals actually imagined they were matchmaking. Well, let them. He knew there was no chance of their succeeding, so why spoil their fun?

Along with the others, he raised his glass of champagne.

The food was everything a bachelor could hope for—hot, delicious and plentiful. Jud went back for several helpings. He noted that Connie ate selectively and drank little, but then, he supposed, that was hardly surprising for such a tiny person.

Jud grew expansive, telling her, with Paul and Helen's frequent interjections, about the log house he lived in.

"When I bought it it'd been empty for years. The place was a mess. Dry rot, mostly. Still, the price was right—"

"And Jud is such a skilled carpenter, he soon had it looking like new," Helen chimed in yet again. What a saleswoman she would make. "Better even. Oh, Connie, you should see it, really."

Connie smiled, silent, as she had been through most of the meal, while the others had talked.

"I was lucky," Jud admitted. "It would have cost me a bundle if I'd had to hire people to do all the fixing. This way all I did was have a plumber out to install indoor facilities and pretty much looked after everything else myself."

"Where did you learn to do all that?" Connie asked. "Surely not at the University of Montana's forestry school?"

"No." Jud swirled the remaining champagne in his glass, watching the bubbly eddies. His thoughts, too, were going around in circles. He was baffled by his behavior this morning. He was talking more than he normally did, but then, Helen and Paul had always been able to draw him out. What was so disturbing was that half the time he was hardly aware of those two—he was talking only to Connie.

Lifting the glass to his lips, he drained it, using the action to cast a glance her way. She sat waiting for him to answer her question. Her expression was one of curiosity, but it also reflected a caring interest that touched a chord inside him.

"No," Jud said again, setting his glass down and turning to face her more fully, "not in forestry school." He grinned. "More like the school of hard knocks, as they say."

"How so?"

"I grew up on a ranch. When things were tight financially—which was often—my father and I would find jobs in town. Any jobs. I served a lot of apprenticeships that way."

As he talked, Jud's eyes dropped to Connie's lips, invitingly full and parted as if in eager anticipation. He wanted to kiss them.

Helen's pointed—and timely—clearing of her throat abruptly pulled him back to reality.

"Paul and I thought we'd stop and visit a friend of ours in the hospital," she said. "As long as we're in Hamilton, anyway. Would you mind coming along, Connie? We'll take you back to Mattville afterward."

Connie seemed at a loss. "Well, I . . . Sure."

"I'd be glad to give you a ride." Jud knew as surely as he knew his name that he was being set up by the Millers. Somehow, though, he could not seem to get worked up about it. Besides, Connie's bewilderment seemed genuine. "It'd be no trouble at all," he assured her. "If you'd rather not go to the hospital, that is."

"Wonderful." Helen was on her feet and tugging on Paul's sleeve before Connie could even form a reply.

"That's settled, then." She gathered up her purse and pushed a partially empty champagne bottle toward Jud. "You two sit a while, enjoy yourselves. And don't worry about the bill. It's been our treat, hasn't it, Paul?"

Paul could do little more than nod and wave goodbye as he was dragged toward the exit by his beaming wife.

Connie watched their hasty departure with more than a hint of consternation. When the Millers were out of sight, she turned puzzled eyes on Jud. "What was that all about?"

Jud decided that telling Connie of his suspicions would only serve to make her uncomfortable. "Who knows?" he said with a dismissive shrug, picking up the bottle. "More champagne?"

"No, thank you." Connie shook her head and frowned, obviously confused. "You know, they never said a thing about a friend in the hospital before. Nothing. In fact, Helen and I had planned a kind of sight-seeing drive through the Stevensville area today. Then this brunch came up—"

"Did you have dinner with them last night?"

Connie nodded, further confirming Jud's matchmaking theory. "Yes, I did. Barbecued steaks and sweet corn. Ambrosia, after two weeks of mostly canned fare and pasta." She glanced at her watch. "If you don't mind, I'd better get back to Rudy. He's not used to being left alone."

"You left him on Butler's Peak with the relief lookout?"

"No, no. He's in my room at the Starbrite. And anyway, as cool and damp as the weather's been, Paul didn't assign a relief."

"Well . . ." Jud drained his coffee, set the mug down and pushed away from the table. "That's bound to change pretty quick now, by the look of today's weather. Things'll be heating up and drying out, and that's when you'll get a chance to earn your keep."

Rising, he held Connie's chair as she followed suit. She bestowed a grin and arched a brow at him over her shoulder, cooing, "Gee, do you think I *can*? I'd better not plan on doing any sleeping at night anymore then, either, huh?"

"Cute, Martinelli." Jud's voice was a growl in the vicinity of her ear as he propelled her toward the exit with one hand firmly at her waist. "We'll see if you're still laughing after you've handled your first fire. Meanwhile, what d'you say you and I pick up that dog of yours and the two of you come over and take a tour of my place?"

"The log house?" Connie stopped walking, as surprised by the invitation as Jud was himself. Eyes wide, she turned to stare at him. "Are you sure?"

Jud shook his head, his gaze locked on hers, his brows furrowed. "No," he said slowly, "I'm not." Then his fingers briefly squeezed her waist and his arm nudged her onward. "But why don't you come anyway?"

Four

With Rudy seated next to her as she drove her Bronco, Connie felt more at ease. The ride with Jud from the restaurant in Hamilton to the Starbrite Motel in Mattville had been something of a strain. What little conversation they had exchanged had been so stilted that she was sure Jud must be having second thoughts about having invited her to his home—just as she was even now debating the wisdom of accepting that invitation. After all, being civil over a meal with mutual friends was not much of a foundation for a more cordial relationship. Intriguing or not, charming or not, Jud Halverson was bound to be the same unpredictable and biased doubting Thomas he'd been the last time they had dealt with each other on a one-to-one basis.

Well, they would see. If he turned into a jerk, she'd leave.

Following Jud's pickup truck at a sedate pace left Connie free to admire the lush mixture of conifers and foliage that lined the highway on either side. No clouds of dust were raised this time to clog her nostrils and coat her skin, thank

God. Having changed from the dress she had worn earlier into white jeans and a T-shirt, Connie had no desire to arrive at Halverson's house looking like the mess she had been after that memorable first drive up to Butler's Peak.

Ahead, Jud signaled left, then turned off the highway onto a narrow road. Following suit, Connie saw a wooden bridge up ahead and through her open window heard before she saw the stream it spanned. Driving across, she noted that the water ran swiftly over a rocky bed with rapids here and there. Cottonwoods stood like sentinels along the bank, as if guarding the house that lay beyond.

Jud was already out of the pickup, watching as Connie drove up. He stayed where he was as Rudy, as always, vaulted over his mistress to be the first one out. Connie followed more sedately. She felt Jud's eyes studying her as she looked at his home.

Connie wasn't sure what kind of vision the term log house had conjured up in her mind—something Lincolnesque and austere, perhaps—but she knew it wasn't the magnificent structure facing her.

Built of stripped timbers at least a foot in diameter each, its two stories gleamed golden in the afternoon sun. A massive porch with comfortable chairs and an old-fashioned swing brought to mind long afternoons spent lazing in its cool shade. It ran along the front and both sides of the house.

Slowly, her eyes continuing their avid inspection, Connie walked toward Jud. Coming to a halt next to him, she managed a grin. "Nice place," she quipped. "Am I in time for the ten-cent tour of the interior?"

"Right on time, ma'am, and for you no charge," Jud tossed back, and motioned her ahead.

Connie stepped onto the porch and trailed her hand lovingly over the railing, which was built of thinner timbers. It was smooth as silk and only faintly abrasive around the knots that rose like arthritic joints in an otherwise elegant hand.

"Knotty pine," Jud commented from two steps below. "Varnished."

"Mmm." She meandered down to the end of the porch and peeked around the corner at the side of the house. Two picture windows faced a bend in the river and a gap in the trees.

Jud stayed where he was, watching her every move. He admired her graceful progress along his porch and was fascinated by the shape of her buttocks encased in white denim designed by Calvin Klein. That Calvin sure knew how to make pants, Jud mused appreciatively, and Constance Martinelli's shape must have been what he'd had in mind when he'd made this particular pair. Yessir, this here was one very fine figure of a woman. As, of course, he had noticed the very first time he'd seen her... and had been striving to forget ever since.

From over her shoulder Connie sent him a smile. "Quite a view from here."

Yeah, Jud agreed silently, smiling back. From here, too. He was glad, suddenly, that he had asked her to come.

He stepped up onto the porch. "Well, come on, then, and see how it looks from the inside. Not that you're exactly lacking for views at the lookout."

Opening the door, Jud savored Connie's scent as he let her precede him into the large entry. "How're you doing up there, anyway?"

"Just great." Connie beamed at her host, not about to confide in him that there were times when the urge to defect still came upon her in the lonely stillness of the night. Or that every shivering sponge bath taken at the cost of numerous buckets of water hauled from the spring had her yearning for indoor plumbing. And that, in addition to her own refusal to be bested, it was the thought of his gloating that kept her on that mountain when stubborn hairy spiders continually insisted on setting up housekeeping in her wallpapered outhouse.

Connie stopped just inside the door to admire the floor-to-ceiling fireplace that constituted the wall in front of her. *"Wow."*

Jud closed the door and squeezed past his guest. Her obvious admiration filled him with proprietary pride.

"You're looking at a fully functional heating unit here," he informed her, stepping up to the hearth and throwing wide the doors in front of the opening. "See, the firepit also opens onto the living room, which means that this baby heats the entire downstairs."

He pointed to the grills on either side, then to another below the door. "This here's the air intake, and here's where the hot air gets blown out. I can control the amount of heat emission by simply turning..."

Jud's sentence ended abruptly. He straightened and offered Connie an apologetic grin. "Uh, sorry about that— I tend to get carried away."

Connie smiled, finding his obvious pride rather endearing. "It's a beautiful fireplace." She touched one of the rocks. "Fieldstones?"

"River rock." Jud, too, placed a caressing hand on the rocks, his enthusiasm resurging. "You should have seen them when I bought the place. Black, almost all the way up to the ceiling. There were times when I was scrubbing the filth off them that I hated every one of those overgrown pebbles. But then I got to love them. No two are alike, you know, just as no two of the timbers in this house are the same."

"And that appeals to you?"

Jud frowned at Connie. "Yes. I like things that are special, not run-of-the-mill. Makes life more interesting, don't you agree?"

Connie shrugged, boldly looking Jud up and down. "That depends. In your case, I'd gotten the impression that you liked everything very predictable and status quo."

Jud, aware that they were no longer discussing rocks and timbers, left the fireplace and stepped around Connie to the curving staircase at the side of the entry. His hand on the banister, he turned and waited until she faced him. "*Some* things, yes."

They stared at each other for what seemed to Connie an eternity. Her heart began to hammer in her chest. Like the rapids in the river outside, her blood was rushing through her veins, only to collect in a hotly churning pool at the pit of her stomach. Pretending nonchalance, she asked, "Women?"

Nonplussed, Jud blinked, breaking the spell Connie had cast on him with just a look. Noting her immediate chagrin at the question, he threw back his head and laughed delightedly. Not about to give her an answer, he turned to start up the stairs.

"C'mon," he said over his shoulder, still chuckling. "I'll show you the rest of it."

Connie wanted to kick herself for having asked such a stupid question and him for being so maddeningly unaffected by her when she seemed to find so much about him to admire. And not just the physical things. Perhaps perversely, she liked the very reticence that so irked her at that moment, just as she applauded the uncompromising honesty that had prompted him to object to her as a fire lookout. Applauded, yes, Connie thought with grim resolve. Accepted, no. Before the fire season was over, she would make him eat those objections.

Forcing her eyes away from the firmly muscled buttocks and lean thighs ahead of her, she followed him upstairs.

Two rooms connected by a large bathroom made up the second floor. One of the rooms was obviously the catchall, judging by the hodgepodge of luggage, baseball parapher-

nalia, stacks of magazines and books piled on and around
a single bed and dresser.

"I don't get many houseguests," Jud commented dryly.

"I can see why." Connie took a perfunctory look around.

Jud chuckled again, appreciating her quick tongue, and
disappeared into his bedroom.

Connie hung back, hovering in the doorway. She liked
what she saw. The room was large, the ceiling vaulted, the
varnished timbers gleaming with the rich patina of seasoned wood. Along one wall maple nightstands, each supporting a lamp whose base consisted of a gnarled piece of
vanished root, flanked a king-size bed covered by a luxuri-
ous patchwork quilt in blues and browns. A large maple
dresser, a desk littered with papers and a well-used recliner
made up the rest of the furnishings.

"Come on in," Jud said, tossing jacket and string tie on
the bed. He undid the top two buttons of his shirt and rolled
up the cuffs. "See the view from here."

He walked over to a glass door on the far wall and, after
sliding it open, stepped out onto a spacious deck.

Connie followed, trying to keep her eyes off the huge bed
and her mind from wondering if anybody shared it with Jud
from time to time. Or, worse, on a regular basis. The ensu-
ing vision was distinctly distasteful, and she was relieved to
step out of the room and onto the deck.

Below lay a yard with a barn and a garage, and beyond it
stretched a green pasture gently sloping upward until it met
with clusters of pines that eventually became dense forest
farther up the mountain. A few head of cattle and two
horses grazed contentedly. The air was mild, though not yet
warm. It was pungent with the earth smells of trees, grass
and manure.

"Lovely," Connie said, and she meant it. She reentered
the room. "Your bedspread is really special, too," she continued, inwardly groaning, as she knew she was treading on
dangerous territory.

"My mother made it," Jud replied.

He seemed blessedly unaware of her wayward imagination, and Connie called herself to order. Stopping in front of the tall dresser, she studied the photographs there.

"Are these your parents?" she asked, indicating a large picture in an ornate frame that depicted a rugged man with cold eyes and a handsome woman whose smile was Jud's.

"Yes, on their thirty-fifth anniversary. My father is dead now." Jud frowned at the picture, his tone curt. It softened when he indicated the other photos.

"And these are my two sisters and their husbands on their respective wedding days. John—" he tapped his fingers against the likeness of the shorter, stockier man "—now runs our family's ranch. The boy is my nephew, John, Jr. But look—" Jud took Connie's arm, none too gently, and propelled her from the room "—you're here for a tour of the house, not an inspection of the family gallery. They're just plain folks, ranchers and farmers. Nothing glamorous."

As Jud hustled her down the stairs, Connie could hardly catch her breath, much less protest that being glamorous had never ranked very high on her personal list of priorities.

"They look like nice people," she managed to say, wondering how she could possibly have offended his sensibilities.

"Hmm." Jud knew he was behaving like an idiot—he seemed to do that a lot around this particular woman—and it wasn't as if he were ashamed of his family, except perhaps his father. But the last thing he wanted from Constance Martinelli was some patronizing comment regarding their plain clothes or their wholesome faces.

They were not in the same league with her or her socialite parents, a fact—God knew—he was only too aware of. Her face might be scrubbed clean today, and her nails no longer manicured and painted red, but that alluring scent of hers still spelled big bucks and high living.

Having asked her to come suddenly seemed like folly again.

"The living room," he said, indicating the large room without his earlier enthusiasm.

He watched Connie marvel at the U-shaped arrangement of the couch and the two loveseats. Covered in cowhide the color of milk chocolate and the texture of velvet, they faced the flip side of the entry's massive fireplace. The skin of a black bear—all four legs spread in apparent surrender, its head almost lifelike as it stared back at her with beady glass eyes—lay before the hearth.

"This is really lovely," Connie exclaimed, trailing her hand over an old steamer trunk that, leather straps and all, served as the coffee table. Two refinished cable reels supported lamps at either end of the couch. "Did you do all the decorating?"

"Yup." What had she expected, orange crates? As with the house itself, he had fashioned or refinished a lot of its furnishings. The maple dining set, his bed, the sofas and the state-of-the-art stereo equipment were pretty much the only things he had bought new.

The picture windows overlooking the forest that lined the bank of the river were like a mural along one wall, while a grouping of Western paintings adorned the one across from it.

Connie recognized two Russells and a Remington, but not the fourth picture. It was of an Indian woman, papoose strapped to her back, standing on a cliff and scanning the watery expanse below. She strained to see the signature.

"It's a Leigh," Jud informed her. "Reproduction, of course." One brow arched as he shot her a sardonic look. "It's called *Return of the War Canoes*. It's a favorite of mine. I love the concept of the devoted wife and mother awaiting the return of her man."

He added a mocking smile to his expression and ushered Connie toward the couch. "Chauvinistic sentiments on my part, I reckon, to your feminist ears. Can I fix you a drink, a cup of coffee?"

"Coffee—and I'm not a feminist in the way you obviously seem to think."

Resisting the subtle downward pressure on her arm, Connie disengaged herself and stepped around Jud. "I'll help."

Jud shrugged. "Okay—but the kitchen is not exactly at its best right now."

Leading the way, he pointed to a sinkful of dirty dishes. "See what I mean?"

He shifted plates and glasses, stacking some on the cupboard so that he could fill the coffeepot with water.

"So, what do you think of the place?"

"Fishing for compliments, Mr. Halverson? Seems to me I've oohed and aahed constantly since we arrived."

Jud grinned. "What is that saying—flattery will get you anywhere?"

"And where is that?"

Jud turned from his task to stare at Connie. Then, with a wry shake of the head, he went back to measuring coffee into the filter. "You're a brat, you know that?"

The way he said it made the words almost a compliment. Connie laughed softly, content with the way things were going.

When the percolator was plugged in and hissing, Jud took her elbow. "Come on, let's go wait on the back porch. Kitchen's no place to entertain a lady."

Connie nodded pointedly toward some wineglasses. One of them was smeared with lipstick.

"Seems you entertain some *ladies*—" she teasingly stressed the term he had used "—very nicely." Had that one slept in his bed?

"A regular playboy, that's me." Jud leaned past her to open the door. "After you, Mrs Martinelli."

Oh, no, not a playboy, Connie thought, stepping out onto the sun-dappled porch. She knew that breed, and Jud could never belong to it.

She settled into the redwood recliner Jud had pulled up for her.

"Your home is beautiful, Jud," she said, leaning back with a contented sigh. "But I must say that after two weeks at the lookout it strikes me as almost criminal that one person alone should occupy a house this big."

A hummingbird, wings beating so rapidly that they were a blur, hovered before a brilliant red geranium and sipped from its nectar. Connie watched in delight.

"Look," she whispered to Jud, unconsciously gripping his hand.

He did. At her. With a peculiar little smile that had the power to hypnotize. The tiny bird was forgotten.

When Jud abruptly disentangled his gaze from hers and turned away, Connie felt dazed, as if she had indeed just come out of a trance. To compose herself, she looked back at the flower, but the hummingbird was gone.

Jud moved a small table closer to her, his face shuttered, and sat down in a lawn chair on the other side of it.

Connie watched him stretch his long legs out in front of him and cross them at the ankles. Neither of them spoke for a while.

"So you feel cramped at the lookout, is that what you're saying?" Jud asked suddenly, out of the blue. "You've had enough?"

Connie's gaze flew from his legs to his face. The question and the hostile tone in which it had been couched startled her. What had changed his mood this time? One moment he was looking at her the way a kid looked at candy, the next he was barely civil.

"When did I say that?" she demanded, thinking that if he wanted a fight—and, judging by the light in his eye, he seemed to—then, by God, she would give him one. "I only said that compared to this—" she paused to wave her hand, indicating her present surroundings "—the lookout is small. And, no, I have not had enough."

"I hear you did some redecorating."

Connie arched a brow. "You mean the curtains?"

"Curtains?" Jud looked thunderstruck.

"Yes, for the windows."

"Windows?" Jud leaned forward to stare at her, aghast. His voice was choked. "You made curtains for the windows?"

"Of course *I* didn't," Connie exclaimed. Did he have to repeat every word she said? "I don't know the first thing about sewing. What I did was give the dimensions to Helen. *She* bought the material and sewed them. Then *I* paid for them and *we* hung them up. Bingo."

Jud was listening to her as if to a lunatic.

"You hung curtains on the lookout windows?" he repeated incredulously, his voice rising. "Woman, don't you realize those windows are bare for a reason? You're supposed to *look out* of them. To spot fires, if it isn't too much trouble."

Thoroughly exasperated, Jud turned his head and glowered at Rudy, who prudently settled himself out of reach at the top of the stairs. *Curtains. Only a city woman would pull a damn fool stunt like that.*

Connie was seething. The man was treating her like an imbecile again. She sat up straight in her chair, the better to look down her nose at him.

"I am well aware of my responsibilities, Ranger Halverson, and the curtains don't interfere with them in the least."

"I'll bet." Jud shot her a glare, then stared off into space again. *Next she would probably put doilies on the fire-finding equipment.*

"In any case, I only draw them at night, for privacy."

"Privacy?" Jud's head whipped around toward her again. "There isn't another soul within miles of you, up, down or sideways."

"I don't care," Connie replied, so primly that under different circumstances Jud might have been amused. "I felt exposed."

Jud gnashed his teeth. The idea of someone watching her undress turned his stomach, which was already churning like a volcano about to erupt from the strain of having her near and yet off limits.

And then Connie added, "And anyway, they make the room a lot homier."

"Dammit to hell!" Jud leapt to his feet as the mountain roiling in his gut exploded. "If you're such a dedicated homemaker, then how come you up and left your husband?"

Connie leapt up, too. "Who said I did?"

"Well, didn't you?"

Chests heaving, nostrils flaring, they faced each other across the small table like combatants in a prizefight. Connie longed to shout at Jud that it was none of his business, that she owed him no explanations, but even through the momentary haze of her inflamed senses she knew that something important hinged on her answer.

She forcibly unclenched her fists and, drawing a deep breath, straightened her hunched shoulders.

"It wasn't the way you seem to think."

"Then how?" Jud, too, made a visible effort to relax.

Connie shrugged, reluctant to say more. Her past was her own, and it was gone. Finished. So was the woman who had been Vincent's wife, and she saw no reason to resurrect either one. Still, if she wanted Jud to like and respect her—and, God help her, she did—some kind of explanation seemed to be in order.

"Things just didn't work out," she finally said, somewhat stiffly. Maybe if she stated things in a brisk and businesslike fashion and kept her emotions out of it it wouldn't be so difficult to talk about it.

"I used to think I was too unsophisticated to keep a man like Vincent interested, but I've long since realized things aren't that simple. I was naive, that much is true—I was only nineteen, after all, when we got married. But I wasn't stupid, and I really worked at being the kind of wife he seemed to want. It was never enough." She shrugged, attempting nonchalance. "Now we're divorced."

"Just like that?"

Connie's short laugh was bitter. "Hardly. It took a while for me to become aware of the problem. And even then I thought if I tried harder..."

She bit her lip and swallowed, angrily shaking her head. Even now, years later, remembering the humiliation and sense of defeat brought the acrid taste of bile into her mouth. When she spoke again, her brisk tone had deteriorated to a pain-filled whisper.

"I'd do silly things like get a new hairstyle, or I'd read *Fortune* magazine or *Forbes* and try to make intelligent conversation. Or I'd buy sexy nightgowns guaranteed to seduce. It didn't matter—nothing made any difference. If he noticed at all, he merely laughed, as if I were some idiot child playing games. In the end..." Connie inhaled raggedly and raised her eyes to meet the angry compassion in his. "In the end, I took what remained of my pride and left."

"Other women?"

"Yes."

Jud's muffled curse was part of a forceful exhalation of air. He pivoted away from Connie and stalked to the porch railing. Supporting himself on two fists, he stared sightlessly at the red-and-white barn across the yard. He could think of nothing to say. He wished he had the right to take her in his arms and tell her that her husband must have been a fool.

For a time there was silence, except for the steady rush of water flowing over and around the rocks in the river at the side of the house.

Jud turned and, folding his arms across his chest, looked toward Connie. They studied each other as if they'd just met.

Connie was thinking how glad she was to have told Jud everything. Apart from Helen, she had never confided in anyone this way. It felt good. *She* felt good. What was Jud thinking, though? she wondered, searching his face, his eyes for a clue.

Jud was troubled. He wished he had never asked about Connie's divorce, for now he had to deal with her answer. Now he understood what had happened and, understanding, could no longer condemn. Condemnation had been one of his defenses against her.

His shoulders slumped, and he pulled his gaze away from Connie's searching one. Burying his hands deep in the pockets of his pants, he studied the tips of his boots. Too late now for second thoughts and wishing he'd minded his own business. Besides, she still wasn't for him. He and this woman belonged in different worlds. All he had to do was remind himself of that from time to time.

"I'm sorry." A crooked smile stretched Jud's lips, though his eyes, when they returned to Connie's, remained somber. "I had no right to ask."

"It's okay." Connie was touched by his obvious distress and strove to lighten it. "Even though the divorce was final only a few months ago, we've been separated for two years now. Whatever hurt there was is pretty much gone. I'm ready to build a new life."

"And where will that be?"

Connie shrugged. "Who knows? I've got résumés out all over the country." She laughed, eager now to reinforce the restored truce. "With luck, some posh private girls' school will make me an offer I can't refuse."

"Yes," Jud said slowly, "I can see you in a place like that."

"Really?" She tilted her head thoughtfully. "I'm not sure I can."

Then she waved the topic away with a gesture toward the sunny day beyond the confines of the porch. "Nor do I want to think about schools right now. It's too pretty a day." She offered her hand. "Come on, let's go for a walk."

Jud seemed to need a moment to switch gears. "What about our coffee?" he asked.

"Later." Connie moved toward the two steps leading down from the porch. "Come on, show me around."

Jud's smile, though slow in coming, was worth the wait. "A walk it is. Just give me two minutes to change out of these Sunday duds."

Connie had walked with Rudy as far as the barn when Jud caught up with her again. "We'll leave the barn for later," he said, falling in step beside her. "First, let me show you my favorite fishing hole. Do you fish?"

"No." Connie tossed him a teasing glance. "I suppose now you're going to tell me I should."

"As a matter of fact, I was. Most folks around here, men and women alike, are quite proficient with a rod. And with a gun, for that matter. I'd be glad to teach you."

"A gun?" Connie frowned at the idea, kicking at a pebble, watching it roll and bounce ahead of them down the path. They were close to the river now, and a foaming rapid was tumbling noisily over some boulders to their left.

"I don't like guns," she informed Jud, her eyes fixed on the spot where the rock had disappeared. "Too many people get killed by them."

"Maybe in New York, but not here. Here we use guns for hunting, and we hunt responsibly. By learning the right way to handle one, for starters. How about it? Want to learn?"

Connie squinted up at him with a grimace. "I'll take a rain check, okay? Now, come on..." She playfully punched his arm. "I'll race you." Her heels kicking up the dust, she ran ahead and down the low embankment.

At the river's edge she set out across some rocks sticking out of the water and, balancing carefully, picked her way to a large boulder near the middle of the stream. She perched on top of it. Looking back at Jud, who had remained on shore, she patted the spot next to her, yelling, "Come on. It's lovely out here."

Shaking his head at her childlike exuberance, Jud nevertheless did as Connie asked. Careful not to get his boots wet, he tested each stepping-stone along the way for stability. He felt a bit foolish tippy-toeing his way into the river like this, more like a kid than he'd felt even when he'd been one. But he shot a furtive glance over both shoulders and relaxed. Who was to see him?

Connie scooted over to allow Jud more room as he lowered his bulky body next to hers. Even so, her shoulder was firmly pressed against the steel of his arm and their hips and legs were mere inches apart. Striving to ignore the tingling heat in the spot where they touched, Connie drew a deep breath, pulled her knees up to her chest and wrapped both arms around them. Her eyes shone with the joy of the moment.

"Isn't this great?" she asked. "Let's pretend we're stranded on this boulder and all these rocks around us are hungry crocodiles just waiting for one of us to fall asleep and slide into the water. So in order to stay awake we have to keep talking. You first," she said with an encouraging grin. "Say something that'll keep me awake."

Jud shifted, trying to get comfortable, trying to get into the game but finding it difficult. Whoever heard of crocodiles in the Nez Perce?

"Say," he groused, shifting again and wincing as a jagged edge dug into his buttocks, "couldn't you have found a bigger and softer rock for us to be stranded on?"

Connie laughed at his aggrieved tone and jabbed an elbow into his side. "Come on, spoilsport," she said, straightening her legs and pushing herself off the rock in one smooth movement, "there's a better one over there."

Surefooted in her sneakers, hopping from rock to rock, she went farther out into the river.

"Careful there," Jud called, following much more sedately, the leather soles of his cowboy boots as slick as ice. "Watch your..."

With a screech and a flailing of arms, Connie landed on her rump in the swiftly moving water as her legs shot out from under her.

"...step."

Jud stared at Connie, who was sitting neck-deep in the river. Her face bore a look of such comical surprise that he started to laugh. Unmindful of his boots now, he stepped into the water and sloshed toward her, all the while loudly giving vent to his mirth.

Nor did he stop laughing when he had reached her. As he leaned over and held out a helpful hand, her narrowed eyes and tightly compressed lips were mere inches away from his face. "Are you all right?" he spluttered.

"Just fine," Connie replied through chattering teeth.

Accepting Jud's hand, Connie let him hoist her up to a crouch, then leapt to her feet.

"Your turn," she cried, giving his chest a mighty shove that sent him reeling.

He clutched at the air, struggling for his balance, and it actually looked as if he might make it when a boulder caught his heel and sent him sprawling with a splash.

Now it was Connie's turn to laugh, and she only wished she wasn't so cold and could enjoy the moment more.

Jud's face was a study in comical male outrage. Yanking his hat from his head, he slapped the surface of the water with it.

"Dammit, woman," he yelled, scrambling to his feet though only after several tries had landed him back on his rear. "Was that necessary?"

"Yes! You were having way too much fun at my expense."

Chest heaving, water streaming off his jeans, Jud stood unsteadily in knee-deep water while his accusing glare turned into a grin.

"You're still pretty funny-looking," he said, his eyes raking her dripping form. When they paused on her breasts, which were tantalizingly displayed by the wet and clinging T-shirt, the grin faded. Without warning, desire replaced every other emotion, fogged his brain and robbed him of words. God, but she was beautiful. A perfectly shaped Dresden mermaid. He ached to scoop her up and crush her to him.

Connie shivered violently and hugged herself, searching for warmth. The movement broke the sensual spell that was holding Jud captive.

"Come on," he said, his voice strangled as it fought its way through his constricted throat. He extended a hand. "Let's get out of here before we catch our death."

Teeth chattering in earnest, feet numb, Connie took a faltering step in his direction and almost fell again. With an oath, Jud reached out and hauled her up into his arms. When she protested, he did what he had wanted to do for weeks. He put his mouth on hers, hard. The contact was brief but electrifying, and it shocked Connie into silence while Jud sloshed back to shore, all his senses clamoring for more.

A warm and dry Rudy greeted their arrival with joy. He jumped around, barking and cavorting like a playful pup as Jud strode toward the house.

Connie wriggled in his arms. "You can put me down now."

Jud tightened his grip. He wasn't about to let her go so soon.

"Be still," he ordered gruffly, adding in the direction of the dog, "You, too. How come you're not wet like the rest of us fools, anyway?"

"Rudy doesn't like the water," Connie informed him.

"Smart dog."

Jud crossed the porch and set Connie down near the kitchen door. She briefly leaned against him for balance, and Jud, feeling her body against his like a searing brand, wondered why his wet clothes didn't sizzle from the heat. He let go of her arms as if burned and stepped back.

"I've got to get these boots off before I go in the house," he murmured. The words sounded foolish and inane to his ears when inside he was such a mess of conflicting emotions. "They're full of water."

He struggled to do so while Connie untied the laces of her sneakers and stepped out of them. As she slipped off her socks, her eyes went to Jud. He had gone to the edge of the porch and hooked the back of his heel on it in an effort to pull off the boot. He was not having much success.

"Let me help you." Connie went to one of the lawn chairs. "Sit down here and I'll pull them off."

Jud was reluctant to do as he was bid, but he complied. He stretched out one leg. Connie straddled it, picking up his foot and presenting him with a view of her trim backside that inflamed him anew. Swallowing hard, Jud closed his eyes.

"Now," Connie ordered, pulling, while Jud placed his other foot on her rump for leverage. Foot and boot smoothly parted company.

"Where'd you learn to do that so well?" Jud asked without opening his eyes as he and Connie repeated the procedure of push-and-pull with feet reversed.

Stumbling slightly as Jud's second foot was abruptly released from the boot, Connie upended it to pour out the
water and tossed it down by the other one.

"My grandfather was a rancher, and the only thing my
mother liked about that was horses. So I always had one to
ride, even in Chicago."

Connie straightened and squeezed excess water from the
hem of her T-shirt. "I told you once, you don't know me,"
she added. "You still don't."

Less than an hour later, Connie was wrapped in Jud's
bathrobe and toasting her toes in front of a blazing fire.
Comfortably reclining on the bearskin, her upper body
propped against the couch, she was balancing a cup of coffee on her stomach and dreaming into the flames.

Her thoughts were on the kiss they had shared, all too
briefly, in the river. She remembered the shock she had felt,
the current of electricity that had jolted her to the marrow.
Had it been like that for him? He hadn't let on, though the
way he had looked at her just moments before had had her
shivering from more than just the cold.

Restless, Connie sat upright and drained the last of her
coffee. It was strong and bitter, and she gave a small shud-
der of distaste as she set the mug aside.

"Still freezing?" Jud had appeared with silent tread and
joined her on the rug. He angled his bare feet, which stuck
out from a clean pair of jeans, toward the fire before drap-
ing an arm across Connie's shoulder. Gently he drew her
against his side. "Here, let me warm you."

Wide-eyed and questioning, Connie turned her head, only
to find Jud's face scant inches away from hers. His breath
was a hot caress that dried her lips, making it necessary for
the tip of her tongue to moisten them.

As he watched her, fires ignited in the turquoise clearness of his eyes, and her heart turned over. There it was, she

exulted, the blaze she had longed to rekindle. Bathed in it, she melted against Jud like beeswax in the sun.

"Your clothes should be dry in about half an hour," he whispered, tightening his grip on her shoulder and looking at her mouth. "Then you can leave and get up the mountain before dark."

Connie struggled to swallow and breathe. "Good," she said shakily, though she wanted nothing more than to stay where she was forever. And to be kissed again, she added, raising her lips to his.

Five

The kiss began as a light, exploratory touching of lips, a mutual discovery of tastes and textures. They nibbled and savored, nipped and traced, until at last their mouths merged with passionate impatience.

Jud savored Connie's sweetness and delighted in the softness he found. He told himself to keep it light, to stop and pull away. He didn't. Couldn't. Not just yet. He drew her closer, coaxed open her lips and deepened the kiss with the play of his tongue.

He gave up trying to convince himself that she was nothing special. Because she was…just as he had known, feared, she would be. She tasted sweeter than caramel candy and smelled as good as sunshine on clover. She felt good in his arms. She felt right.

Fiercely he gripped Connie's head with his free hand and held it captive. He slanted his lips across hers hungrily and thrust his tongue into the hot sweetness of her mouth, again and again. He was on fire.

It took but a moment for Connie's desire to match Jud's. Shaking, every bone and sinew in her body turning to liquid, she responded to his demands and made some of her own with hands that teased and caressed the smoothness of his muscled back and shoulders.

Caught up in their embrace, they toppled onto the bearskin. Their legs intertwined. Stroking and searching, Jud slipped his hand into the gaping front of Connie's robe. She strained toward him, and he cupped the firm breast she offered for his touch. Gently he smoothed and fondled it, tracing a finger across its peak.

The kisses they shared seared Connie's very soul, and murmurs of protest escaped her lips when Jud relinquished them to bury his face in the curve of her neck. His breathing was ragged, the groan he uttered tortured, and Connie delighted in the knowledge that he shared the powerful emotions that rocked her.

Reaching up and burying both hands in the rich fullness of Jud's hair, Connie tugged until he lifted his face from the cradle of her neck and shoulder and looked into her eyes. His were like sparkling crystals, bright with desire.

"I want you to make love to me, Jud," she whispered, emboldened by that look, and by the caresses they had shared.

The words seemed to echo in the suddenly charged silence. Passion flared in Jud's eyes and stole Connie's breath, but then he closed them with an agonized groan and shook his head. "I can't."

His movements jerky, he pulled away from her and sat up.

Connie lay unmoving, uncomprehending. The pleasurable feelings of moments before reduced to a churning ache in the pit of her stomach, she stared at the heaving, well-muscled back he presented her with.

"Why?" she asked softly. "Did I do something . . . ?"

"No." Jud raked a hand through already-tousled hair and violently shook his head once more. "It's not you. It's ... I just can't."

His hand dropped, and his shoulders slumped. "I'm sorry."

So much pained self-recrimination reverberated through the rough timbre of Jud's voice that Connie's forehead smoothed. Why, that poor man ...

She sat up and scooted closer to lay a gentle hand on his shoulder. "Please, Jud, it's okay," she said softly. "If there's a problem ... I mean, I understand if you aren't ... can't ..."

"What?" Jud's head whipped around, and he stared at her, aghast. "What're you trying to say?"

"I'm saying that I know there are times when a man can't quite ... you know ... when he's ..."

This was so embarrassing. Connie cleared her throat and tried again. "When he's—"

"No!" A hard hand swiftly covered her mouth and cut off the rest of the word. "Don't even think it."

Male outrage, then dismayed amusement, showed on the craggy face before her. With eyes gleaming and relentlessly locked on hers, Jud shifted his position, caught one of Connie's hands in his and pressed it into his lap. "Feel that?"

"Oh!" Surprise—first at his action, then at the unmistakable evidence of his arousal—gave way to shock. Connie felt a hot rush of blood swamp her neck and cheeks. Her wide-eyed gaze clung to Jud's with something bordering on desperation. She heard as much as felt her heart beating in her chest with all the speed and resonance of a drum roll, and all the while her hand lay snuggled against—

Connie snatched the tardy hand away as if burned and tried to marshal her scattered wits. "I—"

She broke off to clear her throat and moisten her parched lips. Even so, her voice was little more than a creaky whisper when she finally managed to speak.

"I think we should talk about this, don't you?"

Jud's brows rose a fraction of an inch, all traces of amusement erased from his expression. Connie thought she saw regret, chagrin and even a grudging respect in the clear brilliance of his eyes as he gave a weary nod. His "Yes, I think we should" was part of a ragged sigh.

Moving with a fluid grace that Connie couldn't help but admire even now, he got to his feet. Keeping his back to her, he arched his spine and tipped his head to contemplate the beamed ceiling, as if the words he had such trouble formulating were written there.

"I wish to hell none of this had happened," he said, sounding weary. His head dropped forward, and he reached up to massage the back of his neck. "It's all my fault. I—"

"No, it isn't." Her sympathies aroused by his obvious distress and self-disgust, Connie scrambled to her knees and reached for his hand. "I wanted—"

"Don't." Jud moved out of reach and pivoted. His face was grim, his jaw set. "Only children think wanting is all it takes to get something, Mrs. Martinelli. We're not children." He stared down at her, troubled, searching for words. "We have to take responsibility for our actions. I guess I forgot that for a while. Connie, I can't—I *won't*—get involved with you."

"I see." Connie reared back, quivering with hurt pride and humiliation. "Would you care to tell me why?"

"It would serve no purpose, Connie." Jud gentled his tone, hating himself for having gotten them into this mess. "I don't want to make things any worse than they already are."

"Oh, but I insist," Connie spit, an inner devil prompting her to goad Jud into losing the rigid control he seemed so good at exercising while her own emotions ran amok. "Don't stop now, Ranger Halverson. You're on a roll."

"All right." Contrary to Connie's impression, Jud's hold on his feelings was tenuous. At her words, her derisive tone, he let go.

"You want me to spell it out?" he said through clenched teeth, his voice low as he stuck his face almost into hers. "Fine. How about you're too young, too spoiled and too obviously on your way to a better time?"

"Ah, yes, I see." Connie leapt to her feet, and Jud straightened, too. She pulled his robe tightly around herself and faced him with eyes aflame. "I'd forgotten what an excellent judge of character you are."

"Good enough to know you don't belong here."

"You had me all figured out by the second time we met, didn't you? I'm amazed you even asked me here today, me being such a worthless city person and all."

"Believe me, I wish I hadn't," Jud said heavily, the heat of battle cooling just as rapidly as it had ignited. What was he doing trading insults with this woman? This woman who, only short minutes before, he had held in his arms and longed never to let go?

His hands dropped from his hips, and he lifted one of them toward Connie, intending to touch her shoulder in a gesture of conciliation. "Look, Connie, please..."

She flinched. "Don't touch me."

Jud let the hand drop. "I want to explain how it is with me. I—"

Connie interrupted him, turning her back. "I'd like to leave now. Where are my clothes?"

Jud ignored the question. "Listen a minute, will you?"

"No. I get the picture, thank you." She started to walk away, but in one giant stride Jud was standing before her and gripping her shoulder.

"Connie, get off your high horse and hear me out. It's important."

"You can talk, Ranger Halverson, but you can't make me listen. I've heard enough."

Connie tried to shrug off his hands, but without success. So she turned her head and stared at the wall, determined to play deaf.

"I want to tell you I'm sorry, okay?" Jud caught her chin and forced her to look at him. His voice softened, lowered. "I lost my head because I'm attracted to you—in spite of the things I said. Kissing you...God, touching you was special, Connie, something I've never—"

Abruptly he caught himself, jerking back the head that had begun moving toward her, irresistibly drawn even now. He released her shoulders and stepped back, grim again.

"There's just no room in my life for someone like you. Can you understand that?"

"No, I can't," Connie cried. "But don't worry, it couldn't matter less. Now I want my damn clothes."

Furious with herself because it did matter, Connie marched off in the general direction of the kitchen.

Jud, looking murderous, stormed past her and into the small laundry room. "They're right here. Listen, I—"

"I don't want to hear any more." Connie proceeded to yank items of clothing from the dryer, tossing aside any that were his.

Jud swung away but stayed at the door, one raised hand holding its frame in a white-knuckled grip. "I want to get married."

"Bully for you." Connie glared briefly at the smoothly tanned expanse of broad, bare back. What did she care about his matrimonial plans, except to feel sorry for the unlucky bride? She shook the wrinkles from her jeans with excessive force.

"Marriage is a big step for a man to take. He has to be careful, make the right choices."

"Good luck." Connie slammed the dryer door.

Jud hit the doorjamb with the flat of his palm, cursing his inability to make her understand. He was trying to be open with her, trying to salvage some vestige of friendship he'd thought they could share. Turning, he opened his mouth to try again, but the words got stuck in his throat.

Connie was shedding his robe. As he watched, dry-mouthed, it slid off her shoulders to the floor and, stark naked, she bent to pick up the bits of fluff that passed for underwear. Apparently oblivious to the fact that he was watching, she stepped into them with all the panache of a seasoned stripper.

Jealousy slammed into his gut like a fist as Jud reasoned that quite a parade of men must have passed through Connie's bedroom for her to be so casual about nudity.

Pretending not to notice Jud's scowling regard, Connie concentrated on getting her clothes on as quickly as possible. She was determined not to be unnerved by his hovering presence, but her fingers shook as she zipped her jeans. She fumbled her way into the T-shirt and struggled to squeeze her feet into still-damp tennis shoes, all the while almost bursting with the need to escape this untenable situation.

Haste made her clumsy. When she bent to tie her shoelaces, one of them promptly broke and became the proverbial straw that had done likewise to the camel's back.

She snapped upright and marched over to where Jud hovered like a vengeful Viking. "I hope you got an eyeful, Raymond Judson Halverson, because it's the last you'll ever see of me. My condolences to the future missus."

And with that she shouldered past him to storm from the room with one sneaker flopping noisily.

Jud pivoted. "So you're running back to the city, are you?" he called after her.

Connie skidded to a halt in front of the fireplace and whirled to face him. "You'd like that, wouldn't you?" she flung back. "If only to justify your opinion of me. Well,

I'm staying, Mr. Ranger—but I don't have to see *you* to do my job.''

And with that she rounded the corner of the hearth and was gone with the slam of a door. Jud heard her call sharply to Rudy, start the engine of the Bronco and roar out of his yard with tires squealing. It wasn't until all was quiet that he spun around and rammed his fist into the nearest wall. The pain felt good.

Connie barreled out onto the highway and didn't slow until she hit an unseen pothole with such force that she was almost catapulted through the roof of her vehicle.

"Ouch!" She slammed on the brakes and jerked to a stop at the side of the road. She sat for a minute and concentrated on breathing, not even aware of the tears that coursed steadily down her face. It wasn't until her breath caught on a sob that she muttered a broken "Oh, hell" and let her forehead fall onto the hands still clutching the wheel.

She abandoned herself to the tears that were welling up, letting them drip from wrist to lap in a deluge of grief. Riding the crest of this sorrowful tide was the flotsam of her hurt pride and injured dignity. The sting of Jud's rejection and the bite of unfulfilled desire still gnawed at her innards.

"Louse," she mumbled, sniffling. "Blind and stupid idiot."

Rudy edged closer and laid a comforting head on her shoulder. Connie sniffed again, and the flow of tears slowed. She squeezed one hand into the pocket of her jeans and fruitlessly searched for a tissue while the other one patted the dog.

"It's okay, Rudy," she mumbled, giving him a final pat before using both hands to grip the hem of her T-shirt and wipe her dripping face. "I guess I'm the idiot, aren't I, for wasting even a single tear on that man. He doesn't want me in his life? Fine. Did I say I wanted to be in it?"

She dropped the shirt, staunchly telling herself she had only lost her head for a while and that if she never saw Halverson again it would be too soon.

With the gears grinding in protest, she slammed into first and wobbled back onto the road. She couldn't wait to get home.

Home. Incredibly, the word conjured up her room at the lookout. After parking the Bronco, Connie hurried toward it as if toward a sanctuary. For the first time since her arrival a couple of weeks ago she was genuinely grateful for the solitude that awaited her.

She was barely breathing hard by the time she balanced her load of supplies on one knee and unlocked the door. Physically she was in great shape these days.

"Thanks for small favors," Connie muttered, thinking that that was not much of a reward for the disaster this summer was turning out to be. At the present rate, more than just her manicure would be devastated forever.

In spite of her grousing, Connie took pleasure in noting the changes she had made since taking possession. True, the furnishings were the same ultilitarian monstrosities they had always been, but the addition of her own things had added color and warmth.

Her books were leaning drunkenly on the shelves and ranged in content from the philosophical to the concrete. Hegel, Thoreau and Dr. Seuss rubbed elbows with Steinem, Gurley Brown and Ludlum, while James Herriott's animal stories and the *Guide to Rocky Mountain Wildflowers* cozied up to volumes of romances. As with most things, Connie's taste in literature tended toward the eclectic and shifted with her moods.

Pots of geraniums, gifts from Helen and Paul, added vivid splashes of scarlet and green to the institutional whiteness of the place. Here hung an artfully draped cloth, there, on her cot, lay splashy, bright pillows. The controversial curtains were tied back to serve as narrow, multi-hued frames for the spectacular 360 degrees of alpine view.

It even smelled like home, Connie thought with satisfaction as she inhaled the mixed fragrance of her own scent, pine needles and last week's cooking.

She set her burden on the washstand and checked the buckets. One was full, the other nearly empty. Connie filled the enamel bowl and the teakettle, then stepped back out onto the porch. There she filled Rudy's dish with the remainder before hurrying down the trail for the rest of her things, as well as a fresh bucket of water.

All the while she took care to keep her thoughts away from Judson Halverson, succeeding until much later, when she lay in her bunk and listened to the rhythm of Rudy's untroubled sleep.

The events of the day sneaked up on her then, flickering like a B movie. She saw Jud at the brunch, ruggedly handsome in his Western shirt. She felt again his touch, his kiss, and longed to be able to change the script of the day's events. She remembered his plans for marriage and gave the pillow a vicious punch.

Jerk, she thought, and, exhausted both in mind and body, she slept.

Jud did not. Frustration such as he had not experienced since adolescence consumed him. Images of Connie's lovely body performed exotic dances in his head and drove him crazy. Why did the woman have to come into his life just when he had things all figured out? he ranted silently. And why in the name of baled hay couldn't Kris Morgan fire him up like that city woman could? Connie made him laugh, she made him mad. And, if today was anything to go by, she made him crazy.

With an oath, he reached over to snap on the bedside lamp. Blinking against the sudden brightness and cursing again, he sat up. He would never get any sleep tonight.

He propped his elbows on drawn-up knees and rubbed his
face. How the hell was a man supposed to be fit to work in
the morning? As he struggled to bring order into his jum-
bled thoughts, he craved a cigarette for the first time in
months and wished he hadn't given them up. Reminding
himself that it had been for his own good did little to soothe
him right now. He was feeling acutely aggrieved and de-
prived and generally not too good about himself.

Jud threw back the covers and got out of bed. Stepping
into his clothes, he thought of how tough it had been to stop
smoking. But he had done it, by damn. Could denying
himself the pleasure of Constance Martinelli's delectable
body and diverting company really be that much more difficult?

Jud heaved a sigh and headed for the barn. It sure as hell
looked like it.

Two days later Connie was at the spring, shampooing her
hair beneath the piece of hose, when Helen arrived in a
cloud of dust. Resigned, Connie waited till it had settled and
rinsed again. The water had not warmed en route from
whatever glacier had spawned it, and it made Connie's scalp
tighten painfully while she gasped and squealed beneath the
icy stream like a demented otter.

"Nice to hear you singing so early in the day," Helen
quipped, picking Connie's towel from a nearby branch and
handing it to her.

"Cute." Connie grimaced and fashioned a turban, eyeing her friend with disfavor. "What brings you here—as if
I didn't know—and what took you so long? I expected you
yesterday, panting for information."

Undaunted by her friend's lack of welcome, Helen
grinned and hooked a companionable arm through Connie's as they walked slowly up the trail.

"I would have been here, but I couldn't get away. Which
is just as well, since some mail came for you in the after-

noon. From School District Number Ten, in Washington State—but forget that for now. There's also—''

"Forget that?" Connie said, stopping in her tracks. "I'll have you know that's my future you've got in your bag there. The very first reply to the résumés I've sent out." She disengaged her arm and held out her hand, palm up. "Gimme."

Helen sighed with dramatic exaggeration but pulled the letter from her purse. "Here, but I also have—''

"My first response. Let it be good." Connie snatched the letter from Helen's hand and ripped it open. She hastily scanned the few typewritten sentences, then whooped.

"They want me to arrange for a personal interview."

"Great." Helen's enthusiasm was perfunctory. "I want to hear all about it, but I've been trying to tell you, there's a letter from Vincent."

"Vincent?" Connie jerked back, staring blankly at her friend. *"Vincent?"*

She accepted the letter gingerly, then dropped it as if it were something live and slimy. "I don't want to read it."

"Connie!" Helen tossed Connie a look of fond reproach and bent to pick it up.

"Leave it," Connie snapped.

"Don't you want to know what he wants?"

"I know what he wants. I just don't know why he wants it." Connie stared with distaste at the letter on the ground. "He was bugging me for weeks before I could make my escape and come here."

"After all this time? Why? What about?"

Connie didn't answer right away. She bent, picked up the letter and, straightening, tore it into little pieces. Clutching the shredded paper in a tightly closed fist, she turned to march up the path.

"You ready for a laugh?" she called back over her shoulder to Helen. "He claims to regret all that has passed between us and wants another chance."

"No!" Helen, panting, was incredulous. "What did you tell him?"

Connie shot her a wry look. "Guess."

Helen gave a brief laugh. "Right. Why did I even ask?" Then she looked worried again. "But shouldn't you have read the letter? What if—"

"No way. I've got enough headaches right now without the likes of Vincent Martinelli—"

"Headaches?" Helen said. She stopped walking and grabbed Connie's arm to keep her from moving. "What headaches? Something happened with you and Jud, didn't it? What?"

Connie glared into Helen's expectant face. "Don't mention that name to me again. Ever."

She pulled her arm out of her friend's grip and raced up the path with Helen chasing and calling after her.

"Wait! Connie! What happened?"

Their arrival at the lookout was a dead heat, with both of them panting. They dropped down on the bottom step of the stairs.

"Okay," Helen wheezed, "without mentioning names—what happened?"

"In a word, nothing. And I may never forgive you for your part in the whole mess."

"But—"

"No. No buts." Connie jumped to her feet, tossed away Vincent's torn-up letter and yanked the towel off her head. "I know there was no sick friend in the hospital. You deliberately set me up to go with...with that *ranger*. Well, I want you to know it was a low-down, rotten stunt to pull."

She stormed upstairs.

A little later, however, she and Helen were sitting on the lookout's only two chairs across the small table from each other, drinking coffee. Helen had managed to wring a censored and abbreviated recital out of Connie, who had secretly been glad to air some of her hurt and disillusionment.

Helen looked thoughtful as she contemplated the contents of her cup. "I'd say you're a threat to his peace of mind and he's scared of you," she finally declared.

Connie's mouth dropped open, and she stared speechlessly. Then she hooted.

Helen was unperturbed. She raised her cup and sipped coffee until Connie quieted. "I'm serious," she said then. "You stir something in him. That much was plain even in the restaurant. Personally, I think you'd be perfect for him, Connie..."

"I don't want to be perfect for him, dammit."

"...just what he needs." Helen took no notice of Connie's exclamation. "But it won't be easy to make *him* see that. Hmm..." She thought for a moment. "What exactly do you feel for him?"

"Supreme dislike and acute irritation about sums it up," was Connie's retort. Then she sighed, shaking her head. "Who am I kidding? I find him more attractive than any man I've ever met."

She paused to frown into space. "He's honest, *honorable* in that cockamamy way of his, I suppose. He's...I guess 'manly' is the word I want. You know?"

Helen nodded and managed a leer. "Oh, yes, I know. I'm married, not dead."

Connie spared an absent chuckle for her friend's humor, but her thoughts remained focused on Jud, conjuring up his image dressed in nothing but faded jeans. Definitely manly, and, to her, maddeningly sexy.

"Of course, he doesn't talk very much and is way too serious most of the time, but I suppose that's better than Vincent and most of the other men I've come in contact with. Except for my father, they always talked too much and too smoothly—always ready with a line and a clever comeback."

She grimaced with remembered distaste, and Helen laughed. "Pretty speeches are not Jud's forte, as I guess you've found out. But he's not without humor, either, once a person gets past that reserve of his."

Connie thought of Sunday and had to agree. He'd dropped the reserve, and then...

"Well, it doesn't matter," she said. "Regardless of what you say he feels for me, I doubt he'll do anything about it. And don't you try to, either, Helen Marie Miller," she added fiercely, gripping Helen's arm. "I mean it. I'll never speak to you again if you do. I have a whole new career ahead of me, and I enjoy being in charge of my own destiny. I neither want nor need a man in order to feel fulfilled, you got that?"

"Right," Helen said sarcastically, peeling Connie's fingers off her arm and rising to carry her cup to the washstand. "And far be it from me to tell you otherwise. Oh, I almost forgot..."

She set the cup down and went to get her purse from the shelf by the door. She withdrew several small envelopes and handed them to Connie. "The seeds you wanted. Now, show me where you planted those strawberries, and then I've got to run."

At ten o'clock the next day it was already well into the eighties. If there was a wind, it lacked the energy to stir things up.

Connie, clad in a halter and matching pink shorts that had looked darling in I. Magnin's summer display but were not nearly as cute when paired with steel-toed hiking boots and knee-high socks, wished she was at a beach somewhere.

Instead, she was hacking with a hoe at some unyielding soil she hoped to transform into a small garden. On the ground next to a watering can, a bag of fertilizer and an assortment of tools lay Helen's packets of seeds. The colorful pictures on the envelopes promised a splendid mixed salad in about six weeks.

Connie straightened to wipe her brow with the back of a gloved hand, adding to the smudges of dirt already there. Stretching cramped muscles and rolling her shoulders to limber them up, she squinted against the glare of the merciless sun.

Suddenly she tensed. Her shoulders stilled, her eyes strained to clearly see the wooded slopes across the valley.

Could it be...?

Connie swallowed against the scratchy lump of fear that suddenly closed her throat. She blinked to clear her vision.

Was that...?

She was running up the stairs before the thought completed itself.

Was that smoke? Oh, God, was there a *fire*?

Connie grabbed the binoculars from where they lay on the bookshelf and rushed to the window. Adjusting the focus with trembling fingers, she scanned the wooded hills.

Yes, there it was. Smoke—black, curling billows of death and destruction, tainting the pristine clearness of the Rocky Mountain air.

Six

For several heartbeats—an eternity—Connie stood mesmerized, unable to do anything but stare in morbid fascination. Her pulse was racing, and her heart throbbed painfully.

Her mind was a blank.

As she watched, frozen, a second longer, a larger cloud of smoke burst into the air. Connie thought she could all but hear the crackling of the flames that spawned it and smell the acrid stench of burning brush. *Fire!*

The word screamed in her brain and galvanized her into action. In two long steps she was at the table that supported both the telescope and the azimuth. Her thoughts focused on the task at hand and feeling fully in control, she switched the radio to channel 3 and was hailing the district dispatcher even as she scrambled up onto the high stool and aligned the telescope.

"Mattville dispatch, this is Butler's Peak. Over." Connie repeated the call, all the while busily noting coordinates, locating landmarks and striving to estimate wind speed and direction.

"Mattville dispatch, Franzen. Go ahead, Butler's Peak."

At the sound of Steve Franzen's voice, Connie lost her tenuous hold on professionalism and spluttered, "I see a fire. There's a fire across the valley."

There was a short pause, and then a midly amused sounding Franzen replied. "You have a *smoke*, Butler's Peak? What is its location?"

"Located in the direction of Deer Creek." She forced herself to be as cool as the dispatcher was. "Azimuth 110 degrees. Section 14, township 28N."

"Can you see the base of the smoke? What is its position on the slope?"

"Negative on the base. Position is lower third on a fairly gentle slope. Pretty close to Deer Creek Campground, in my estimation."

"Fuel?"

"Grass and brush, I'd say, given the location and smoke coloration."

"Size?"

"So far, not much more than a spot, but spreading as I watch. Smoke is fairly heavy in volume and drifting northeast, so wind direction southwest at about 4 or 5."

"Okay." Franzen no longer sounded amused. He spoke crisply. "We'll get on it pronto. Since there hasn't been a thunderstorm, and given the location, it sounds like a careless camper. Lucky for us the area is easily accessible, and we should have things under control pretty quick. Keep an eye on it in case anything important changes.

"Good work, kid. Be sure to fill out the fire-detector report and file it. Over and out."

Connie leaned down and, with a trembling hand, switched the radio back to channel 1. Then she slumped on the stool and buried her face in her hands, momentarily overcome in the aftermath of reporting her first fire. *I did it,* she thought, dazed. *I spotted the thing, reacted swiftly and reported it correctly. I did it!*

Whooping, she jumped off the stool and ran to press her nose to the window. There it was, she marveled with something close to pride of ownership.

She ran out on the porch. "Rudy! Did you see what I did, boy?" Dropping to her knees beside him, she held his head to make him look in an easterly direction. "See? I've just single-handedly saved one of the nation's national forests."

Jumping up, she smiled from ear to ear. "Wait till Jud Halverson hears about *this*. I'll bet..."

Her smile fading, Connie stood still. "Damn." She stomped her foot in a childish but satisfying display of temper, thinking how infuriating it was to have her thoughts constantly straying like lost and lovesick ewes toward that particular ram.

She didn't care, Connie reminded herself sternly, taking up the binoculars to keep an eye on the fire's progress. She didn't care if the ranger heard about her fire or not. Of course, he would—but she did *not* care! The man had spelled out to her the fact that she meant less than nothing to him. She neither wanted nor needed his approval.

Her conviction was put to the test when, several days later, while making a quick, unscheduled dash into town for some fresh victuals, Connie ran into Jud in Mattville's supermarket.

It was their first encounter since that fateful Sunday. In fact, it was Connie's first time off the mountain in the three weeks since then. With the dry spell they were having, every lookout was on special alert, and she had gladly forgone her days off for overtime duty. After all, what was waiting for her in Mattville but heartache and aggravation?

And there was Mr. Aggravation himself—and impossible to avoid. Just as it was impossible to keep her foolish heart from doing flip-flops at the sight of all that tall and rugged masculinity. Damn.

Connie thought of fleeing, of forgoing fresh ground round and sticking with canned corned beef hash, but Jud had spotted her and was watching her with that poker-faced expression he used to hide his thoughts. That stiffened Connie's backbone. Did he think she was playing hooky from work? Technically, she supposed, he could say she was—there was no relief person up at her lookout. But then, she only planned to be gone a couple of hours, tops, and she *had* cleared it with Paul.

She marched over to Jud with chin raised and shoulders squared. "Well, hi, Mr. Ranger, *sir*," she said smartly, like a buck private saluting a superior officer.

She'd been expecting him to scowl, and she was disconcerted to see Jud's rugged features crease in a grin. Humor brightened his beautiful eyes.

"Don't you start with me," he told her while she stood and basked in the warmth of his gaze. "How've you been?"

Before Connie could formulate a reply or even think to warn herself that this was merely the warm side of Jud's habitual hot-cold cycle, Joe Benson, the butcher, held out a large package. "Here you go, Jud. Anything else?"

Connie thought she saw regret at the interruption darken Jud's eyes before he turned to accept his purchase. She told herself not to be silly. Certainly his tone betrayed no untoward feelings as he said, "No, thanks, this'll do it, Joe."

Connie placed her own order and tried to come up with some chatty comment, only to hear herself blurt, "So...did you hear about my fire?"

Jud's smile widened, and Connie's knees lost their starch at about the same time her mind was erasing every thought but the one that pleaded, *Please, God, give me this man, even if just for a little while.* She was proud to note, though, that her hand was steady when it picked up the package of hamburger meat Joe had wrapped for her.

"I suppose Paul told you," she continued, dropping the hamburger into her cart but seemingly unable to likewise drop the topic of their conversation.

Jud walked with her to the produce section. "Paul, Steve, Helen . . . even Elsie," he replied. "They're all pretty proud of you."

Connie, though her blood was quickening in her veins, managed to hang on to her wits sufficiently to keep from asking, *"And you?"*

They stopped in front of a pyramid of Golden Delicious apples and faced each other. Connie wondered if maybe her eyes were asking what her mouth had had the sense not to put into words, because Jud looked at her with unmistakable pride and softly said, "Good job, Connie. You're quite a woman, and a damn fine lookout. I guess I owe you an apology."

There was not a thing Connie could think of to say, and the lump that was suddenly clogging her throat would have made speech impossible anyway. All she could do was stand there.

"I've got to get going," Jud said.

Connie nodded and managed a smile. "Me, too."

Neither of them moved.

"Excuse me, Jud. Begging your pardon, ma'am. Could I play through a minute?" A burly, grizzled rancher grinned amiably and touched a finger to the brim of his hat as he pushed his cart through the opening Jud had created by stepping away from Connie.

The spell that had bound them was broken, and Jud glanced at his watch. "I've really got to run." He hesitated. "I, uh . . . I guess I'll be seeing you."

Connie nodded, her vow to banish him forever from her thoughts forgotten. With emotions running the gamut from the ecstatic to the bereft, Connie stood and watched him talk with Gert, the checkout clerk, and pay for the meat. He left the store without once looking back.

Look what we've got for you:

5 FREE GIFTS

... A FREE bracelet watch
... plus a sampler set of 4 terrific Silhouette Desire® novels, specially selected by our editors.

FREE MYSTERY GIFT

... PLUS a surprise mystery gift that will delight you.

All this just for trying our Reader Service!

If you wish to continue in the Reader Service, you'll get 6 new Silhouette Desire® novels every month—before they're available in stores. That's SNEAK PREVIEWS with 10% off the cover price on any books you keep (just $2.24* each)—and FREE home delivery besides!

Plus There's More!

With your monthly book shipments, you'll also get our newsletter, packed with news of your favorite authors and upcoming books—FREE! And as a valued reader, we'll be sending you additional free gifts from time to time—as a token of our appreciation for being a home subscriber.

THERE IS NO CATCH. You're not required to buy a single book, ever. You may cancel Reader Service privileges anytime, if you want. All you have to do is write ''cancel'' on your statement or simply return your shipment of books to us at our cost. The free gifts are yours anyway. It's a super sweet deal if ever there was one. Try us and see!

*Terms and prices subject to change without notice.

Get 4 FREE full-length Silhouette Desire® novels.

Plus
this lovely
bracelet
watch

Plus
a surprise
free gift

▼ PLUS LOTS MORE! MAIL THIS CARD TODAY ▼

Silhouette's Best-Ever "Get Acquainted" Offer

6 FREE GIFTS 6

Return This Sticker
and Get 6 Gifts—FREE
Compliments of Silhouette

Yes, I'll try Silhouette Books under the terms outlined on the opposite page. Send me 4 free Silhouette Desire® novels, a free bracelet watch and a free mystery gift.

225 CIS JAYW

NAME _____

ADDRESS _____ APT. ____

CITY _____

STATE _____ ZIP CODE _____

Don't forget...

...Return this card today and receive 4 free books, free bracelet watch and free mystery gift.

...You will receive books before they're available in stores and at a discount off the cover prices.

...No obligation to buy. You can cancel at any time by writing "cancel" on your statement or returning a shipment to us at our cost.

If offer card is missing, write to: Silhouette Books
901 Fuhrmann Blvd., P.O. Box 1867, Buffalo, N.Y. 14269-1867

BUSINESS REPLY CARD

First Class   Permit No. 717   Buffalo, NY

Postage will be paid by addressee

Silhouette® Books
901 Fuhrmann Blvd.
P.O. Box 1867
Buffalo, NY 14240-9952

No Postage
Necessary
If Mailed
In The
United States

Connie inhaled a long, shaky lungful of air and wondered if Helen could be right. *Did* she stir something in Jud, as her friend claimed? There were times when she thought she did. Like today.

She wasn't vastly experienced where men were concerned. Vincent had been her first real love, and she'd married him at nineteen. During her lengthy separation from Vincent she had had neither the time nor the inclination to pursue romance. Yet, in spite of all that, she wasn't so naive that she couldn't tell when a man was attracted to her.

Jud Halverson was attracted to her.

The thought caused a glow until she remembered that he himself had admitted as much. She sighed, kicked the cart and shoved it toward the lettuce. Back to square one.

Jud's mind was not on driving as he headed back to the ranger station in the forest-service pickup. It was on the perky little handful of female he'd all but fled from back in that supermarket, had been on her ever since he'd had her over to the house.

What was it about her? he asked himself for the umpteenth time since first clapping eyes on her in Elsie's office. It wasn't as if she were a raving beauty, though she certainly was easy on the eyes. And it surely wasn't her charm, since most of the time they spent together she was spitting at him like a cat whose fur he'd rubbed the wrong way.

Jud passed the Starbrite, touching a finger to the brim of his hat in reply of Elsie Slater's and Maveen Wilson's waves of greeting. Gossiping, he reflected with a mental shake of the head, catching sight of them in the rearview mirror with their heads together again. Who and what did they always find to talk about?

A wry chuckle escaped him. Other people's business, of course. And wouldn't they have a field day with the feelings Connie Martinelli stirred up in him?

Jud accelerated, out of town and on the highway now for the last miles to the station complex.

Gossips and small towns went hand in glove, but so far he had always managed to avoid being the subject of Matt-ville's supper-table and across-the-fence talk. Nor did he intend to change that. No, sir. All he had to do was stay clear of Butler's Peak and its occupant and keep to himself the fact that he couldn't get her off his mind.

Gravel crunched beneath the pickup's tires as Jud swung the vehicle off the highway, into the wide drive leading through a stand of mixed conifers and up to the cluster of log buildings that comprised the Mattville ranger station. The drive forked, and Jud kept to the left, driving into the parking area in front of the building that housed the administration offices.

He pulled into his customary spot, reached for his pack-age of steaks and got out.

It was a sunny day, though on the muggy side, and wind-less. Still, the scent of freshly mowed grass, of firs, and ce-dars and pines, as well as the shadows they cast, created an illusion of coolness. Insects buzzed more maddeningly than usual for the time of day, but the birds were silent.

A storm was brewing, Jud thought, noting with half a mind the unfamiliar flashy sports car parked near the door of the building. The other half was thinking that he hoped the storm would bring rain. Fire hazard was high right now.

Inside the building, walking through the small public area, Jud spotted the driver of the fancy car. Had to be, he thought with amusement; the guy looked just as fancy. Della, one of the clerks, was talking with him across the counter, and Jud didn't stop on his way to his own office in back until she hailed him.

"Ranger Halverson."

Jud's brows rose at her unaccustomed formality. He stopped and turned around. "Yes?"

The visitor was flushed with annoyance, Della with exasperation. "This man won't tell me what it's about," she informed Jud with some heat, "but he insists on speaking with you."

"Oh?" Jud shifted his gaze to the stranger, who straightened away from the counter and moved toward him. "What can I do for you?"

"Are you in charge here?" the man drawled, looking Jud up and down with somewhat condescending curiosity.

Jud returned the look with a measuring one of his own, unruffled by the inspection. He suspected that in his less-than-pristine uniform he failed to measure up to the other man's standards. In a three-piece suit and a nice tie, hair neat and shiny, he looked like the guys pushing underwear in magazine ads. A salesman? Disgruntled tourist? Neither assessment seemed to fit.

"I'm District Ranger Halverson," he said, figuring that introductions were the best way to find out who and what his visitor was all about. "You wanted to see me?"

"I want the man in charge. If that's you, then maybe we're getting somewhere."

"What can I do for you, Mr.—?"

"Martinelli. Vincent Martinelli." He pulled a small leather wallet from his jacket pocket, extracted a card and handed it to Jud. "I'm here about my wife. I understand she works for you."

Jud stood without moving, his eyes riveted on the card in his hand, then slowly lifted his head to stare at the visitor. *So this is the husband.*

He took stock of the man again, this time noting the obviously expensive cloth and perfect cut of the suit, the tasteful silk tie.

"Let's go into my office," he said, turning to Della to hand her his package. "Put these in the icebox, Della, will you? And remind me later to take 'em home. Thanks."

With a nod toward Martinelli, Jud walked away, leaving it up to the man to follow or not. His mind was in turmoil, his gut was churning and his pulse was racing, but he let none of that show.

"Have a seat," he said when they were inside his office, indicating the cowhide-covered armchair that fronted the massive oak desk. He sailed his hat toward his three-footed coat tree without checking to see if it landed on the hook or not and settled in his own chair behind the desk. He waited for the other man, who was now busy sizing up the room, to speak.

"Nice place," Martinelli said at last, actually looking impressed.

"Thanks." Jud loved it himself. The rich patina of the golden log walls, the shelves full of books and the collection of guns and rifles—some mounted on the walls, some locked in a large oak cabinet that had been his grandfather's. But right now he had no stomach for hollow social amenities.

"About your, uh, wife..." he said, almost choking on the word as Connie's face hovered before his mind's eye.

"Yes. Connie," Martinelli said. "You know her, I expect?"

"Yes. Though she's not, strictly speaking, under my supervision," Jud said tightly. "Is there a problem?"

"Well, yes—I suppose you could say that." Martinelli gave a little laugh, chagrin in his voice. "A lover's spat that got out of hand. My fault, I'm afraid."

He met Jud's hooded gaze with one of disarming humility. "I'm here to mend fences, and to fetch her back where she belongs."

Jud had told himself he should be glad to hear this, but he was numbed by the terrible sense of impending loss. He should be happy to see a broken marriage mended, and the woman who tempted his every resolve and filled him with such unattainable longings gone. He should be relieved.

"She's at Butler's Peak," he said. When he rose from his chair, he felt physically sick. "I'll have Della draw you a map."

A couple of hours after her encounter with Jud in the supermarket, Connie maneuvered the Bronco to a smooth stop near her spring. Gone were the days of the engine stalling and the gears grinding. By now she had become quite a competent back-road driver, and the four-by-four was a familiar friend.

"Rudy, are those motorcycles over by the path?" Connie squinted through the dusty windshield while Rudy ignored the question and tried to get his nose closer to the packaged meat on the back seat.

"Dirt bikes," Connie announced, setting the brakes. "Looks like we have company."

She didn't even try to alight ahead of Rudy, but sat back and waited for him to jump across her lap and out. As soon as his feet hit the dirt, his nose was to the ground, and then he was running toward the bikes.

Connie got out of the truck and leaned into the back seat to gather the two bags of groceries into her arms. Kicking the car door shut with her foot, she followed the busily sniffing dog. She looked forward to greeting her visitors.

Whenever she had to be away for more than a few minutes, Connie locked the place up, but ordinarily all the lookouts had an open-door policy. Visitors were welcome to come inside the building and look things over, and Connie always took great delight in explaining the various instruments and their purpose to her guests.

In return she had had her picture taken with people from every part of the country, it seemed, and several visitors had even brought gifts. She was still enjoying the jar of homemade blackberry jam a woman from Portland, Oregon, had brought her.

Hurrying up the path, arms beginning to ache as they cradled the sacks containing fresh fruit, vegetables, meat and eggs, she was startled by Rudy's sudden, vicious growl. He usually liked visitors as much as she did. Her amazement grew as she watched him shoot up the hill like a rocket.

Connie stopped walking and strained to see what had set him off. He had reached the lookout now and was alternately snarling and barking at someone on the porch.

Something was wrong. Alarms going off in her head, Connie clutched her burdens tighter and started to run. At the foot of the stairs she collided with a person making a hurried exit from her home. The impact sent her sprawling beneath a shower of produce and knocked the wind right out of her.

She lay, gasping and dismayed, as the culprit made good his escape, and she still hadn't moved when an instant later a second person came barreling down the stairs. This one was dragging a determined Rudy, whose teeth were firmly implanted in his pant leg.

Without slowing, they used Connie's prone form as a stepping-stone.

Moments later, wincing as she struggled upright on her abused backside, a horrified Connie watched the intruder stop running and deliver a forceful kick with his booted foot to the side of Rudy's head. As if feeling the pain herself, Connie flinched and gasped. Rudy yelped, releasing his captive, who immediately took to his heels.

Her own sore spots forgotten, Connie leapt up and ran toward the inert form of her dog. "Rudy," she called, a sob escaping along with his name as she dropped to her knees and cradled his head. Eyes closed, his breath coming in shallow pants, he seemed to be stunned or unconscious.

"Oh, Rudy. Rudy." Her tears dropped onto the handsome features of the Doberman, features that, in Rudy's case at least, masked a gentle soul. Connie held him close and rocked him, crooning. In her anxious state it seemed like hours before Rudy's eyelids flickered and finally opened, but when they did she sobbed again, with relief this time. She rained kisses all over his face.

As if embarrassed by this lavish display of affection, Rudy gave a sharp bark and struggled out of Connie's arms. Once free, he was off down the trail.

Sure that by now his chase would be fruitless, Connie stood and turned toward the lookout. Her feet dragged. She fought the urge to run down the trail, get in her truck and drive away rather than face whatever mess awaited her inside.

She barely spared a glance for the spilled groceries as her eyes lit on a bright red object halfway up the stairs. Closer inspection revealed it to be a baseball cap, unfortunately without any kind of team logo. Still, Paul might be able to use it as a clue.

On the porch shards of glass crunched beneath her feet. The window next to the door had been smashed so that the intruders could reach inside and open it.

Connie's heart beat like a tom-tom, loud and fast, and she hardly dared to breathe as she tiptoed across the threshold and onto more pieces of glass.

She stopped and took a careful look around. Relief flooded her. The instruments looked unharmed, the radio untouched, and the rest of her things were pretty much as she had left them. Except for a few books on the floor and the spilled contents of her cookie jar, it seemed the vandals hadn't had time to do any real damage.

Feeling braver and infinitely grateful to the powers that had orchestrated her timely return from town, Connie picked up the mike and switched on the radio.

"Gonzales," she said when the call was answered. Her throat was dry, and she coughed to clear it. "Is Paul or, uh, Ranger Halverson there?"

"Negative on both counts, Butler's Peak. What's up?"

Connie told him, adding, "Nothing seems to have been stolen, but one of the windows needs fixing."

"Are you all right, Martinelli?" Gonzales's obvious concern warmed and comforted her.

"A little shaken." Connie looked at her scraped palms and absently wondered where she had put the antiseptic spray. She scanned the shelves for the first-aid kit as she described what had happened.

She concluded her sketchy description of the culprits. "Teenagers, I'd say. One of them lost his hat, but if there are any identifying marks on it, I can't see them. The other probably has torn pants and Rudy's teeth marks on his legs. I'm sorry I can't give you more information, but it all happened very quickly."

"Well, don't worry about it. As long as you're okay. Do you want me to send someone and make sure they're gone?"

"Heavens, no. I'm fine," Connie protested, with more good manners than conviction. She would have been glad of some company right then, but admitting it seemed rather cowardly. Maybe Gonzales would insist.

He didn't. "Well, if you're sure," he said. "Someone'll be there by noon tomorrow, latest."

Connie nodded as he went on to tell her once more not to worry.

"Right," she said, nodding again. "Sure. I won't. Over and out."

With a sigh, thinking that it was easy for someone at the station to tell her not to worry, she replaced the mike and went to look for Rudy.

He was trotting up the path, his tail, what little there was of it, clamped between his legs and his head drooping in an attitude of dejection.

"I know how you feel, boy." Connie scratched his ears and bent to gather up her scattered supplies. Except for some dirt and a couple of cracked eggs, they were as good as new.

Connie, on the other hand, was feeling decidedly dented. After locating her first-aid supplies, she ladled water into the enamel bowl with hands that shook. Her knees were none too steady, either, and her head and backside throbbed.

As she tidied herself as best she could, her eyes were drawn to the jagged hole in the window and then beyond it to the bank of black clouds that sat like an evil genie's turban on top of Wahoo Peak, across the valley. She became aware of how hot and oppressive the air had become and scooped up handfuls of water to bathe her face and neck. She didn't know when, but she was sure there would be a storm. The thought did nothing to cheer her.

Connie buried her face in a towel and wished she could stay like that for a while, ignoring the world ostrich-style.

When the first loud call of "Hello, the lookout" reached her ears, Connie yanked the towel from her face and stared, incredulous, mouth agape, out at the path.

It can't be, she thought, her heart plummeting all the way to her toes like a runaway elevator before backing up to settle in her stomach with a sickening lurch.

It is! Her caller's identity was clear even before the man hurrying up the path came fully into view. Connie squeezed her eyes shut, then quickly opened them again, hoping she might merely have suffered an optical illusion. She had not.

"Connie?" Footsteps sounded on the stairs, then a short rap on the open door. "Anybody home?"

Connie stared at Vincent Martinelli, who was framed by the doorway. She was at a loss as to what to do or say, as surprised and overcome as she would have been witnessing the Second Coming. Her attorney had handled things when it had finally come down to divorce, and she hadn't seen Vincent in two years. She had thought—hoped—never to see him again. And most certainly not on top of a mountain in Montana.

And yet there he was, incongruously attired in a gray three-piece Brooks Brothers suit, an oxford-cloth shirt and a prep school tie. Blond hair a little mussed from the breeze, the handsome, boyish face a touch flushed from the heat and the climb.

Clutching the towel like a weapon, Connie stood unmoving, her gaze fixed on the man who had once been the most important thing in her life. How long ago that seemed. How far she'd come since then, in every way.

"What? No words of welcome for the loving husband?" Vincent entered the room uninvited and came to stand in front of Connie. He looked down at her with raised brows. "You look like hell."

His sarcasm, so well remembered, prodded Connie out of her reverie. "What are you doing here?"

"Why, I just happened to be in the neighborhood," Vincent quipped lazily, turning to survey the room and sweeping an arm at the view surrounding them. "And quite a neighborhood it is, too. If you're a mountain goat, that is. Not a setting I would have envisioned for you, however."

He dropped his arm and returned his attention to Connie, who watched his every move with fascination. What a ham he was, really, she thought. Every move was calculated for effect.

"What on earth are you playing at here, Heidi of the Alps?" he was asking. "I couldn't believe it when Anna told me what you were up to and where you were."

"Ah, Anna." So it was her mother who had told him of her whereabouts. No doubt Anna had thought his letters and this visit would be the perfect tools with which to remind Connie of all she had given up by divorcing Vincent. So what if he had been unfaithful? Men *would* have their fun.

Connie folded her arms across her bosom and leaned a hip against the washstand. Listening to Vincent's cultured, faintly bored tones, she was glad he no longer had the capacity to impress her.

"Why are you here, Vincent?" she asked, having decided to ignore his baiting. "What do you want from me?"

The coldness of her voice seemed to cut him to the quick. Vincent looked stricken. "I need an excuse to see my wife?"

"*Ex*-wife, Vincent. Capital *E* capital *X*."

He smiled his most charming smile. There had been a time when Connie had melted at the sight of it, and even now it almost had the power to coax a responding one onto her reluctant lips. Almost—but the memory of all his betrayals was stronger.

"Semantics," Vincent murmured, reaching out to stroke Connie's face. "You used to love me."

"A long time ago, Vincent, and not anymore." Connie moved to avoid his touch, dropping her arms and walking past him to stand near the door. It was clear to her that Vincent wanted something beyond that second-chance nonsense he had been bothering her with lately, or he wouldn't have come all this way. He wouldn't go to so much trouble for any woman, least of all her, if something more than his idea of love weren't involved.

But, for the life of her, Connie could not figure out what that could possibly be. Since he was here, though, she intended to find out.

"Please say what you've come to say and leave," she told him coldly. "It's been quite a day, and I'm very tired."

"My, my, how we've changed." Vincent's voice lost its soothing quality and became mocking once again. "It must be the company you are—or aren't—keeping these days. They say too much solitude will unsettle the simple mind, but that doesn't appear to be the case with you. Yours seems to have gotten sharper—as has your tongue."

He folded his hands behind his back and paced, eyes fixed on his dusty Gucci loafers. "Very well, I'll lay my cards on the table."

Connie clenched her teeth, disgusted with his theatrics, and went to perch on the stool by the azimuth. Rudy wandered in from his exploration and, seeing Vincent, growled.

Vincent stopped pacing and stared at the dog. "Call him off me, Connie."

Connie stifled a laugh and called Rudy to her side. "Don't worry, Vincent," she assured her visitor with heavy sarcasm. "Rudy has excellent taste. He's fussy about who he bites." She petted the dog, and he settled down. "You were saying?"

Vincent tossed Rudy another suspicious look, then focused on Connie. "I want us to get married again."

"Oh, *please*!" Connie jumped off the stool and planted herself in front of her former husband. "Don't insult my intelligence any more. Either tell me what you really want or get out."

"I just told you," Vincent said. "And what is more, I think you'll accept my proposal."

"You can't be serious."

"Oh, but I am." Vincent looked smug. "One year, tops. Strictly business, of course. What do you say?"

Connie's eyes narrowed. "Why?"

"What do you care? You'll be amply rewarded."

Connie advanced a step, her teeth clenched. "Why, Vincent?"

"Oh, for pity's sake." Vincent, looking pained, rolled his eyes with patent exasperation. "You always were a drag, and I see that nothing has changed. I thought you grew up?"

He stood with both hands stuffed into his trouser pockets, head lowered, jiggling coins and glowering at Connie, who—happily—remained completely unmoved. There had been a time when this very stance had had the power to reduce her to tears, but no more. Now it only made her smile as she once again strode to the door. "Goodbye, Vincent."

"You know, Constance, this newfound aggressiveness ill becomes you," Vincent snapped, "but all right. My grandmother has finally promised to sign her twenty percent of Thurston Investments stock over to me. I don't need to tell you I want those shares and will do almost anything to get them. Combined with my existing thirty-five percent, they will give me control at last. The catch is, you and I have to 'bury the hatchet and make up,' as she puts it.''

He snorted. "She always did have a soft spot for you."

"And I for her." Which was something of an understatement, Connie thought, remembering the tower of strength and maternal love Prudence Thurston had been to her in the past. "Which is only one of the reasons I'm turning down your ludicrous proposition."

Livid, Connie rounded on Vincent, hands on hips. "You have a nerve, coming up here and thinking I would ever be a party to something so completely underhanded." She pointed a rigid finger at the door. "Get out."

"Now just a minute—"

"Out." Connie's voice rose, and her pointing finger shook. "Get out before I set the dog on you."

Vincent, his hands balled into fists, his handsome features distorted into a mask of frustration, stalked past her, but stopped on the porch.

"You haven't heard the last of me, Constance. I always get what I want, and I want that stock."

"Ooooh!" Beside herself with rage, Connie slammed the door shut. A shower of glass fragments tinkled to the floor as the remainder of the broken window caved in under the force of the slam.

Rudy whined and cowered, and Connie, looking at his pitiful form, started to laugh and cry all at once. Her entire body shook as though with fever and, exhausted, she slumped back against the door.

"Oh, God," she groaned, burying her face in her hands and letting herself slide slowly downward to the floor. "What next?"

Seven

As it turned out, "next" was Deputy Sheriff Ray Gunther, ostensibly to conduct an "investigation into the destruction of government property," as he put it. By that time it was close to eleven o'clock the next morning.

Before going to bed the night before, Connie had decided that now that she knew what Vincent was after she would be ready for whatever other surprises he might plan to spring on her. After that she had banished him from her mind and had gotten a surprisingly good night's sleep. And, having gone without her dinner, she had made herself a substantial breakfast of bacon and eggs.

Dressed in cutoff Calvin Kleins and a tie-dyed tank top, she poured the deputy a cup of coffee and went back to washing the breakfast dishes.

"God, it's hot." Ray removed his hat and mopped his brow with the back of his hand. Plopping down on a chair, he propped his right ankle on his left thigh and parked the hat on his knee. Nodding in the direction of the damaged windowpane, he said, "The vandals do all that?"

Connie grimaced and shook her head. "I'm afraid I did some of the damage when I slammed the door after another unwanted visitor."

"Oh?" The deputy looked intrigued. "Heard tell in town that your husband came to fetch you back to New York."

"Vincent is not my husband," Connie protested, "and I have—"

"According to Elsie, he plans to be again real soon."

"What?"

Ray blew at his coffee and took a careful slurping sip. "Nothing like a hot drink on a hot day, my mama always said. Best thing for thirst." He nodded toward the broken window again. "I take it the two of you didn't see eye-to-eye, then."

"Hardly." Connie emitted an inelegant but expressive snort. She dried her hands on a tea towel and poured a cup of coffee for herself. "And just to avoid any other wild rumors, let me tell you right now that I have no intentions whatever of going back to New York with him. I have a job here, and I intend to do it. And after that—"

"Well, that certainly is a load off my mind." Jud Halverson, his voice dripping sarcasm, joined the conversation. He'd arrived as silently as the hunter he'd once told her he was.

Wide-eyed with surprise, Connie watched him cast a quick glance at the shattered pane next to the door before stepping across the threshold, saying, "I expected to see your bags packed and ready to go, Mrs. Martinelli." His gaze shifted to the deputy. "Hi, Ray."

While Connie stood by the stove, momentarily incapable of more than speechless astonishment, Jud pushed past her and sat down on the chair across the table from the deputy, whose eyes were darting back and forth between the two of them.

"I'll have some of that coffee, thanks. Lord, it's hot."

He, too, removed his hat, but sent it sailing across the room to land on Connie's bunk before wiping his brow.

"Bound to storm," Ray remarked between slurps of coffee. "What brings you up here?"

Connie had been asking herself much the same thing, wondering what, if anything, Jud's presence here meant. Could worry about her well-being have been the catalyst, or had he come to glower and gloat while she, presumably, packed her bags to leave with Vincent? Jud's reply was noncommittal and offered no solution to the riddle.

"Same thing that brought you, I guess," he said to Ray. "The window."

Connie handed Jud her own mug, freshly filled. Two cups was all she had, which, ordinarily, was quite sufficient.

"Thanks." As he accepted the drink, Jud's eyes were clear and bright as they met hers. They betrayed none of his thoughts, yet Connie was left with the feeling that while the storm outside might just be starting to brew, inside Jud one was already raging. The thought was oddly exhilarating.

"Didn't think a little thing like vandalism would bring the district ranger himself runnin' up here," Ray said into the charged silence, lumbering to his feet with a wheeze. "But since you're here, Jud, no sense me hanging around, too. You'll handle things well enough, I reckon."

"The only reason I'm here myself is that the glass needs replacing and there wasn't anybody else we could spare to do the job today. Paul took sick. Flu or something."

Ray nodded, accepting the explanation without comment, but Connie, all her senses sharpened, caught the hint of defensiveness that Jud tried to mask with a gruff tone of voice. Coupled with the increasingly disturbing intensity of their visual exchange, it set her pulse to pounding.

Jud rose, but release from their prolonged eye contact did nothing to slow Connie's heart rate. She watched him round the table, clap a hand on the deputy's shoulder and steer him to the door. Just short of it, they stopped, and Ray turned to smile at Connie. "Thanks for the coffee."

Connie managed an almost-natural smile in return. "Don't be a stranger," she told him. "Visitors are welcome anytime."

"Gotcha."

Arms folded across her bosom as if to shield her vulnerability, one hip leaning against the stove, Connie braced herself for whatever Jud might have to say when he returned from seeing the deputy out. But, braced or not, she was hardly prepared when Jud, stern-faced and silent, crossed the room in four long strides and hauled her shocked and unresisting body against his own. She opened her mouth in a reflexive protest that drowned, unvoiced, in his hotly possessive kiss.

Connie struggled to tug and untangle her arms from between their bodies, needing to press closer. Without thought of what or why, she rose on tiptoe and, clutching Jud's back, molded herself to his muscular frame. Gasps of pleasure formed in her throat as his tongue teased her lips until she parted them more fully and let him in.

"Oh, woman..." Jud's murmur was agonized. He slid one large, callused hand down Connie's back to cup a firm and rounded buttock and lift her more fully into the cradle of his loins. "...what you do to me."

The state of his arousal was evident as he rubbed and rocked against her, and the hand sliding up beneath the tank top to caress the satin skin of her unfettered breasts shook.

Connie was on fire. Her legs reduced to putty, she grasped his shoulders and clung to him for support. At this moment she wanted nothing so much as to sink to the floor and turn into reality the facsimile of the mating act their bodies were performing.

Jud's arms tightened one last time and let go. The hands that only moments before had stroked and fondled spanned her waist and set her several inches away from him. The

strength of Connie's grip on Jud's shoulders hardly less-
ened as she reluctantly opened her eyes to encounter the
turquoise flames burning in Jud's.

For several heartbeats they gazed at each other, and
Connie marveled at the wealth of emotions that sprang to
life within her. As if in response to similar feelings, Jud
groaned and pulled her to him again. This time he held her
gently, as if she were some rare and precious object that
might break if not handled with care.

"You can't leave," he whispered, nuzzling at the sensi-
tive skin below one ear. "I won't let you. I can't. There's too
much we haven't resolved...."

He moved his mouth over Connie's jaw, nibbled at her
throat and worked his way back to her eager lips. They
kissed again, deeply, endlessly.

At length, Jud drew back, his hands in her hair holding
her face up to his. "It's been hell," he ground out. "I
haven't had a moment's peace since that Sunday at my
place. Connie... God help me, I need you. I want you so."

Connie pressed close to silence him with a kiss. "I'm
yours, Jud," she whispered against his mouth. "Believe me,
I'm yours."

She sensed Jud's withdrawal even before he lifted his head
to look into her eyes. A chill crept down her back when he
asked, in a voice as dry and rough as desert sand, "Are you,
Connie?"

She let go of his shoulders, needing distance, but the
hands framing her face held her in place. "What do you
mean?" she asked.

"Your husband came for you. He wants you back in his
life—back where you really belong, Connie. He's giving you
a second chance—"

"To hell with Vincent and his second chance." Connie
knocked Jud's hands away from her face. "Didn't you hear
me tell Ray I'm not going with him?"

She stepped back, heartsick at what she read in Jud's eyes. "You still don't see it, do you?" she said accusingly. "After all that's passed since I came, you still think I'm nothing but a flighty city woman just here for a lark. Just waiting for a better offer."

She pivoted away from him, breathing in loud gasps. Eyes burning with unshed tears, she stared out of the window. The world outside was gloomy, shadowed by a steadily expanding canopy of bluish black that mirrored the turbulence of her own emotions.

"I'm sick to death of being told who and what I am and what I really want," she told Jud in a choked voice. "Of being categorized, labeled and judged. I am *me*—"

She spun around to confront him again.

"I'm a grown person with a mind of my own. I am not the lovestruck nineteen-year-old Vincent Martinelli duped and manipulated at will, and I am not the spoiled and sniveling incompetent you seem to take me for. I can do anything anybody else can, and more than some. And if you, Judson Halverson, are too pigheaded to admit that, then don't come around and bother me anymore."

Jud took two long steps to grip her shoulders. His face was set in lines of stubbornness that Connie was beginning to recognize and heartily dislike.

"The man says he loves you," he told her. "He wants to make amends—"

"He wants to use me," Connie cried, furious with him for being so blind. "He's never wanted me, he's cheated and betrayed me at every turn. How can you think he loves me?"

Jud closed his eyes, pulling her into his arms and holding her tight. He laid his cheek against her hair, asking softly, "How can he not?"

Connie sagged against him, weakened by the feel of his strong, steady arms. "Oh, Jud," she whispered. "No more doubts."

Jud lifted a hand and gently cupped Connie's cheek. "I'll try," he said, his throat constricted. "I'll really try."

They stood like that for long moments, until the sound of distant thunder penetrated the emotion-charged silence they shared.

Jud tensed, lifting his head. "D'you hear that?"

"Yes." Connie, too, was listening intently. "Sounds like the storm is finally moving in."

"Right. And that means I'd better get down to the truck and get the things to fix this window, pronto."

He was out of the door almost before he finished speaking, while Connie still stood as if nailed to the floor. She looked around.

The room was bright with sunlight still, but outside half the sky was obscured by the approaching black and billowing cloud. Slow to break, the storm now seemed to be making steady progress in the direction of Butler's Peak, already blanketing and obscuring some of the neighboring peaks and valleys as it moved. The air was heavy with a sense of impending doom.

She ran all the way to the turnaround, where Jud was just rolling up the window of the forest-service pickup. At his feet lay a satchel of tools and a paper-wrapped rectangular parcel next to a forest-green uniform jacket. His gaze dropped from her face to the pail dangling from her hand. He slammed the door of the truck and grabbed it from her.

"You take the package and my coat," he ordered over his shoulder, already sprinting toward the spring, some hundred feet farther down the road. "I'll catch up with you."

Connie didn't even think about protesting his peremptory manner. She hastened to pick up the flat parcel and hurried back the way she had come.

Jud caught up with her shortly, one hand carrying the bucket of water, the other the bag of tools. "We'd best shake a leg if we don't want to get dumped on."

Glancing up while skipping to keep up with him, Connie had to admit that Jud had a point. Flashes of lightning could be seen now over Wahoo Peak, and thunder, though as yet still faint and distant, rumbled like the growl of a huge waking monster.

It was still sunny on the path, but the sun's glaring light had an eerie falseness and a stinging bite to it.

Connie and Jud wasted none of their energy on words now, but hurried to reach the safety and protection of the lookout. To be caught outdoors on top of a mountain in a thunderstorm was extremely dangerous, especially since at this altitude there were few trees as tall as or taller than they. The sooner they reached the sanctuary of the lightning-protected building, the sooner they would be safe.

All but running up the path, Connie thought she would die of the heat. Sweat trickled into her eyes and blurred her vision with its saline sting. There was no breeze, no twitter of birds, only the maddening buzz of deerflies come to sip the nectar of Jud and Connie's perspiration. Her face set in grim lines, Connie plowed ahead.

At the lookout, she tossed out the cold dishwater left over from the breakfast dishes in the large enamel bowl that also served as her sink at the washstand. She rinsed the bowl, refilled it with some fresh water Jud had brought and plunged her hands into its coolness.

"Come and join me," she said to Jud, who looked as overheated as she felt. "Having your wrists submerged really helps to cool you off."

Their fingers touched. The act of sharing the bowl as they washed their hands and splashed water on their faces created a disturbing sense of intimate domesticity. Neither of them chose to comment on it, however.

Momentarily refreshed, Jud got to work on the broken glass while Connie busied herself pouring lemonade from a pitcher. She brought him a glass.

"Thanks." Jud gulped it thirstily, then wiped his mouth with the back of his hand. "That hit the spot," he said, smiling almost shyly. "Thank you."

Connie smiled into his eyes. "You're welcome."

"Well, back to work . . ."

"Right." Connie was the first to move. She half turned. "I'm thirsty, too."

"Mighty fine lemonade." With visible reluctance, Jud bent to pick up the spatula he'd been working with and returned to the job of preparing the frame for the new pane of glass.

Connie smiled happily to herself and went to have her own refreshment.

After replacing the pitcher in the small refrigerator, she took the binoculars and commenced scanning for fires.

"You know, this is the first electrical storm since I came here," she told Jud. "I thought there'd be more of them."

Jud had removed the remnants of glass still in the frame and was unwrapping the replacement.

"Some years are worse than others, I guess. This has been one of our cooler, wetter summers."

"Well, it's certainly wet all around us now. I can't see a thing out there anymore."

Connie laid aside the binoculars. "I doubt any fire could get started today."

"It'll be pouring rain here any minute now, too," Jud said, darting a look outside. "Can you give me a hand?"

"Sure."

Glad of the excuse to join him at the open door, Connie supported the transparent rectangle the way he showed her, standing on the threshold, one hand holding the panel on the outside, the other on the inside of the door, while Jud smeared putty into the grooves. She couldn't believe they were discussing the weather like polite strangers, but, in her case at least, no other topic came to mind. And, somehow, not talking seemed worse, for then she would be free to speculate on what lay ahead. A storm, Jud here with her...

She inhaled a sharp breath to stem her imagination's molten flow. Close like this, the heat from Jud's body seemed to warm even her bones, and Connie's nostrils flared at the powerful scent of perspiration turned musky and alluring by his brand of deodorant and soap.

"Is there anything you don't do?" she asked, the rapid beat of her heart making her voice sound breathy.

Jud spared her a teasing glance but continued to work putty into the cracks between the glass and the wooden frame without replying.

Connie's already-hot face grew hotter still. "What I meant was—"

"I know what you meant," Jud said with a chuckle. "You can let go now."

As glad as she had been to help, Connie was now even gladder to step aside. She took up a new position several windows over.

"There are all kinds of things I don't know how to do," he told her, scraping and wiping away excess putty with deft and economical motions. "Most of them very important things, as a matter of fact. Things that make a difference in this world. Like painting beautiful pictures, or designing rocket ships. I don't know a thing about poetry, or what makes airplanes fly, radios talk and televisions show pictures. When you come right down to it..."

The job done, he straightened and turned to face her. "I'm just a very ordinary man, Connie."

Connie shook her head. "Not so ordinary, I think."

The moment sparked as their gazes tangled across the room. Jud both wondered and despaired at the riot of emotions that caused every fiber of his being to strain toward her.

The slamming of the door rattled the windows, putting to the test the quality of Jud's work and announcing the arrival of the long-awaited storm. Neither Jud nor Connie noticed the room's increasing darkness until it was briefly dispelled by the flash of lightning. Amid the crash of thunder Connie whirled to stare out of the window into the inkiness outside.

The lookout was like an island in a tempest, with the wind howling around its corners, whipping shrubs and scraggy pines into frenzied undulations. Rain pelted the windows until they were awash with water, distorting the view.

Connie walked to the bookshelf and, after rummaging for a book of matches, lit the thick, ornately carved candle she had bought at a craft fair the year before. Her fingers shook.

Behind her, Jud took up the microphone and called Darby station.

"You staying up there until this thing blows over?" Paul wanted to know, his voice bland.

"Yes," Jud said, "the storm is all around and on top of us now, making the inside of this lookout the safest place on the mountain. There's no way I can leave."

"Right. Over and out."

Jud switched channels and cradled the mike, never taking his eyes away from Connie's. A crash of thunder made Rudy whine and run for cover beneath the table. Lightning flashed, momentarily bathing the room and its two motionless occupants in a bright and silvery light, but the electricity that crackled in the air between them had nothing at all to do with the electrical storm raging outside.

"If you want me to go, I will as soon as things quiet a little," Jud said at last.

Connie, her throat thick, her heart pounding, mutely shook her head.

Jud took a step toward her, then stopped. "Staying, being here with you in the way that I want to, won't be a promise of anything, Connie. I won't ... *can't*—"

He broke off, cursing the honesty that compelled him to spell things out and his inability to do so with tact and finesse. He wished for a politician's way with words so that he could make her see that it wasn't any shortcoming of hers, but fear and uncertainty on his part, that kept him from giving in to the burgeoning feelings in his heart.

"I'd better go."

"Stay." In one swift movement Connie was in front of Jud. Standing close, she tilted back her head in a gesture of invitation as old as time. Framing Jud's face with delicate hands, she pulled it down until their mouths touched at last.

"Stay," she whispered against his lips. "No strings."

The words, the contact, butterfly-light, sent shivers racing down Jud's spine. He shuddered, then closed his arms around Connie's tiny frame, letting his lips and teeth devour her mouth. Their tongues entwined, their hands caressed. It was a kiss of promise and, on Connie's part, a kiss of commitment. Breathless, they drew apart and searched each other's faces, but found only their own yearning willingness reflected there.

Dropping tender, playful pecks across Connie's flushed features, Jud lifted her effortlessly into his arms and carried her to the bunk. One swipe of a booted foot sent his hat flying. It joined Rudy on the floor beneath the table.

Kneeling, Jud lowered Connie onto the bed. With glowing eyes he looked at her, drank in the richness of her hair and shapely brows, the satin smoothness of her face and lips, the enticing perfection of her body.

"You are so beautiful."

Connie reached out a hand and stroked his cheek.

"So are you," she whispered, and she meant it. To her, Jud's face, every tanned inch and leathery wrinkle of it, was the epitome of manly beauty. His body, long and lean and powerful, was as symmetrically perfect and as aesthetically pleasing as any Greek statue. He was honest and forthright; his words were few, but they were chosen with care.

She loved him.

Connie clasped the back of his neck and pressed the length of her fingers into the firm flesh there. "Kiss me, Jud," she whispered, longing and tenderness an ache in the back of her throat. "Please..."

Jud's passion flared, his need exploded. His lips on hers were greedy, all-consuming. He got off his knees and joined her on the bunk, his hands everywhere. Stroking and petting, seeking and finding, they ignited fire wherever they touched.

Connie clung to him, moaning, writhing, as waves of pleasure washed away whatever inhibitions she might have harbored.

"Yes," she cried, clawing at the fabric of the shirt on Jud's back, her hips bucking as his clever fingers found and tantalized the very core of her. "Oh, please... Yes...yes."

The heated waves crested, receded, ebbed momentarily.

Jud kissed the lids of her eyes, sipped from the corners of her mouth, sweetly caressed the skin of each thigh.

Connie floated on a languid sea of contentment, undisturbed by the thunder that rent the stillness with the roar of a thousand cannons and by the psychedelic streaks of lightning that intermittently whitened the candlelit room.

She felt safe and cherished by the man who so tenderly nuzzled her chin, reclaimed her mouth and traced its outline with his tongue.

"Jud," she murmured, stroking the back she had clutched moments before.

"I'm here." Jud kissed her again. "I'm not going anywhere." His hand reached for one of hers, guiding it to his throbbing manhood. "Not for a long time."

"Oh, Jud," Connie murmured, remembering for one fleeting moment the other time she'd felt the strength of him like this. This time, though, there would be no retreat for either of them.

His kiss confirmed that thought. Thrusting his tongue deeply into her mouth, he showed her what he craved. With trembling fingers Connie helped him out of his clothes as he helped her. Skin on heated skin at last, they kissed again, glorying in the sensations the feel of their bodies aroused.

Jud was on fire. Everything within him strained toward this loving woman, this tiny temptress he was holding in his arms at last. He wanted to savor the moment, to prolong the anticipation, to glory in the beckoning fulfillment of his fevered dreams. But her flesh, smooth and soft as the finest satin, was rubbing against his own, urging him to relinquish this last tenuous hold on sanity. Urging him to finally succumb. A ragged moan escaped his throat as, unable now to wait another moment, he positioned himself between her legs and entered her welcoming heat.

Nothing in his life had prepared him for the exquisite sensations awaiting him within; no other woman had ever given him pleasure so acute that it bordered on pain. His mind was filled with wonder, his heart expanded in his chest. There were no thoughts of yesterday, and certainly none of tomorrow. There was only now. There was only this woman. There was only joy.

He tried to be gentle, tried to remember how very small she was, how fragile. But Connie would not have him spare her. Her hands anything but weak, she stroked and clutched his muscled back, urging him on, stoking the fire of their mutual passion until, in one mighty conflagration, their separate selves went up in flames and drifted back to earth as one.

Connie was the first to stir. Moving with extreme slowness she lifted a hand and stroked the fine hairs at his nape.

Jud burrowed his face into the fragrant hollow between Connie's neck and shoulder, nuzzling there. Connie's blissful sigh turned into a grunt as a shift of his body drove the air from her chest. Jud lifted his head.

He rolled onto his back, carrying Connie along. "You okay?"

She nipped at his bristly chin, delighted to be able to do so, to be free to touch him any way she liked. She grinned down at him.

"A little dented, maybe..."

Jud's mouth caught hers in a thorough kiss.

"God, you're sweet," he groaned, his hands exploring her pliant form, taking time to savor each hill and valley as he had not done earlier in his haste to possess her. Lazily he stroked and smoothed the satin of her skin, charting a course for his eager lips to follow.

He kissed her throat, her shoulders, the valley between her breasts. He laved and suckled first one nipple, then the other. Moving lower, he dipped his tongue into the nubby swirl of her navel and delighted in her response to his ministrations.

Connie couldn't believe she could want him again so quickly, but she did. Tremors shook her, and she grasped Jud's shoulders as if they were a lifeline as her hips moved to invite him beneath his persistent caresses.

Jud's lips sought to recapture her mouth, but Connie shook her head, staying his advance with a finger pressed to his searching lips.

"My turn," she breathed between delicate love bites. "I want to learn your body as you learned mine."

Feather-light was the touch of the fingers that caressed and tantalized, exquisite the torture they performed. They found and teased the nipples buried in the mat of grizzled chest hair, coaxed them erect. Her lips followed, soothed them with kisses, while her hand moved downward and searched out an even worthier goal.

Jud groaned from deep within his chest, his hips bucking in reaction to Connie's loving touch. Reaching out, he clasped her shoulders and pulled her up along the burning length of his body until their lips were locked together yet again. Their tongues mating, Connie straddled his narrow hips, and ecstasy beckoned once more.

This time it took longer for them to stir. Replete, they lay entwined and basked in the warmth of their contentment. Connie was nearly asleep, still draped like a blanket across Jud's inert form, when with one mighty roll their positions were reversed.

She opened one baleful eye. Jud was grinning down at her.

She opened the other eye and grinned back. She was happy, happier than she could remember ever having been.

Life was great, the world was bright.

She loved this man.

And he, even if he would not say so, loved her. How else could their joining have been so wonderful, so very special? Throwing both arms around his neck, she kissed him full on the mouth. Nothing fancy, just a great big smack to express the joy she felt inside.

"I love you," she said, and was glad. It felt right to tell him, to say it aloud.

Jud froze, but he resisted the urge to pull away. He knew Connie would misunderstand the gesture, would consider it a rejection. Which, he was honest enough to admit to himself, in a sense it was.

This outpouring of emotion was too much for him. He was unused to touches, kisses, that were meant as mere expressions of affection. To words of love spoken easily in the fullness of the moment. His family was not demonstrative that way, and he was very much the product of their reserved and cautious demeanor. And though he had often envied Paul and Helen their easy affection, now that he was the object of it it made him uncomfortable. It made him feel clumsy and unsure of how to react or reciprocate.

Always before, sex had been...well, *sex*. A form of recreation, release. Fun. But this time, with this woman...

Jud needed space now, a chance to think. A chance to, albeit belatedly, consider the meaning and the consequences of what they had shared. Yet, at the same time, he had better tread easy, lest he inflict new wounds.

After briefly returning the exuberant pressure of Connie's lips, he raised his head and strove for a humorous tone. "D'you hear a loud grumbling?"

Connie kept her hands looped around Jud's neck and her eyelids half-closed. She chided herself for feeling hurt, for having hoped to hear him say, "I love you," in answer to her own spontaneous declaration. Even so, she knew it was too soon for him. *Play it cool. Back off.*

"Loud grumbling..." she murmured, making a pretense of listening. "Oh...thunder, right?"

"Wrong." Jud reached up and gently freed himself from her embrace. "My stomach. The storm outside is over."

He rolled away and was on his feet in one smooth motion. With the same lack of modesty that had so bothered him in Connie that first Sunday, he leisurely assembled his clothes and stepped into his briefs and pants.

Connie, watching with loving fascination, was intrigued by his very brief forest-green briefs. Truly, she marveled, Judson Halverson was a man of many facets.

Catching his glance, she raised her brows. "I like your underwear—it complements your uniform. Service issue?"

Incredibly, he blushed.

Connie, with a whoop of delight, sat up and hugged her knees. Laying a cheek on them, she watched him zip his pants.

Jud, seeing her thus, thought she looked good enough to eat for supper. The immediate flare of heat in his gut both shocked and alarmed him. *Good God,* he thought, *I've just had her twice and already I want her again.*

That was when he knew he was in very deep trouble.

He walked to the tiny refrigerator and peered inside. "You got anything good in here? I'm starved." Extracting a carrot, he eyed it with suspicion. "Is this food?"

Connie jumped off the bunk with an exclamation of concern. "You poor thing, I bet you haven't eaten since breakfast. I know I haven't."

Finding her cutoffs, she stepped into them, not bothering to look for her panties. The tank top she yanked over her head inside out.

"Don't worry about a thing," she assured him. "I'm a terrific cook."

She set about proving it by preparing a memorable feast of spaghetti with her famous marinara sauce, preceded by a more-than-adequate antipasto salad. Concord grape juice was not much of a substitute for a nice, mellow Chianti, but Connie was on such an emotional high that she needed no other stimulation. Nor, it seemed, did Jud.

Over coffee they talked, though—as if by mutual agreement—not about their relationship.

"Teaching school was never anything I had a burning desire to do," Connie confided, swirling the dregs of her coffee into a ponderous eddy. "But when I found myself facing single life again and seriously contemplated a career for the first time..." She shrugged. "There I suddenly was, back in school, majoring in education. Anyway, I like kids. How about you?"

"Sure, I like kids. I play with my little nephew every chance I get."

"Yeah? What do you play?"

"Ball, mostly." Jud's face softened with love, and Connie vowed that one of these days—and soon—he would look at her just that way.

"John plans to pitch in the majors."

Connie whistled, impressed. "And he is how old?"

"Five." They laughed.

"Did you know I was once a den mother?" Connie asked.

"No, but oddly enough, I can believe it. Hell, I bet you were pretty good at it, too."

"Darn right I was. Our den even won the pinewood derby."

"Is that so?" Jud grinned, enjoying their easy camaraderie. "All the judges were probably hankering after one of your pretty smiles and *let* your bunch win the race just so's you'd give 'em one."

"What?" Connie leaned over to punch his shoulder. "Are you saying we didn't win fair and square?"

Jud caught her hand and held it at the spot she'd punched while he snaked his other arm around Connie's waist. With one mighty yank she was off her chair and in a heap on his lap. Connie shrieked a protest, which he stilled with his lips.

"I'm saying you could probably charm the birds out of the trees," he murmured when at last they came up for air. "I know you've turned *my* life upside down."

Neither of them was smiling as, for several heartbeats, they studied each other. Jud closed the small gap between their faces again. But just for the briefest of soft kisses, a mere laying of mouth on mouth.

Still, when it was over, Connie just sat there, eyes closed, content and happy. She was still in a state of euphoria when Jud all but dumped her languid body on the floor and rose.

"Dishes," he pronounced, his voice—in Connie's opinion—filled with an annoying amount of purpose.

He was doing it again, she thought as she watched him fill a pot with water and set it on the stove to heat. He was putting emotional distance between them, as if the closeness they had just shared frightened him. It *did* frighten him; she was sure of that now.

Jud was capable of tenderness and love, out of bed as well as in. He had demonstrated that. All he needed was someone to practice sharing it with on a regular basis.

Connie smiled to herself. She was that someone, even if he didn't know it yet.

"I'll dry," she said, joining him at the washstand. "I'm trying to preserve my manicure."

They both looked at the short, neat but unspectacular nails she held up for inspection.

"Nice," Jud said.

Connie rolled her eyes in mock despair. "Shows what you know," she quipped. "Wash, already."

Jud poured water into the bowl and washed.

Connie polished each piece with excessive vigor. "Somehow I never pictured you doing, quote, woman's work, unquote," she told him.

"Really?" Jud handed her another plate. "How *did* you picture me?"

"Well..." The question was too good to pass up, Connie decided, peeking at him out of the corner of her eye. "To tell you the truth, naked, mostly."

Jud's reaction was everything she had hoped for. He stood with both hands in the dishwater and stared at her. When she burst out laughing, he said sternly, "Have I told you before that you're a brat?"

Connie nodded. "Yup."

Then, unable to do otherwise, she leaned over and kissed him. "You're cute when you're shocked."

"Cute? I'll show you cute." And before Connie knew what he was up to he framed her face with dripping, sudsy hands and kissed her fiercely. Oh, yes, Connie exulted, she was definitely the someone he would practice with.

The dishes done and the storm no more than a memory, they took a stroll around the lookout building and down the path. Overhead, a nearly full moon reigned supreme in a star-studded sky. A gentle wind fanned heated cheeks and carried the scent of freshly washed earth.

Somehow it was understood that Jud would stay the night.

"Nice job of decorating," Jud commented when he emerged from the outhouse. Arms across each other's backs, they strolled up the path, Rudy bounding ahead. "Does the *Wall Street Journal* know that people use them for wallpaper?"

Connie chuckled, pleased by his attempt to temper bewilderment at her decorating urges with humor. "Sure they do. It vastly increases their circulation and gives a person a chance to garner financial savvy without leaving, uh... home. Anyway—" she jabbed an elbow into his midriff, causing a grunt "—you know I don't have the real thing in there. Still, it adds a certain...oh, I don't know...je ne sais quoi, don't you think?"

"Jinny *who*?"

Eight

Jud wished he didn't feel like a cowardly thief sneaking off when the day was barely dawning, but he did.

Connie's face, in sleep as innocent as a child's and snuggled into the depression he had left on her pillow was an indictment. Still, there was no way he could stay, no way he could deal with her and the emotions she stirred in him until he'd had time to think.

Jud perched on the bottom step and pulled on his boots. Connie was so giving, so open, so different in her demonstrative affection from anyone he knew. It was nice, in a way, he reflected, striding down the path. He could probably get used to it in no time.

It wasn't until he stuck his head under the hose at Connie's spring that he remembered that he still hadn't decided there was room in his life for a woman from New York, no matter how affectionate. Or was there? Could he ask her to stay? Should he? And what if she said no? How did he think that would feel?

Now there was a question Jud knew the answer to. Knowing it, he resolved that it was better to leave the other ones unasked.

Gritting his teeth, Jud kept his head beneath the icy flow until breathing became impossible and the chilled tightness of his scalp unbearable. He dried himself on his uniform shirt and turned to leave. He gunned the engine, turned the pickup around and sped away from Butler's Peak as fast as conditions allowed.

Connie's first thought on waking was that her body ached deliciously, each twinge and kink a tactile reminder of the night she and Jud had shared.

Jud. Connie's head popped up off the pillow, which still held his scent. She squinted against the brightness.

"Jud?"

Rudy strolled over to give her arm a desultory swipe with the tongue, but for once Connie did not acknowledge his morning greeting. She was busy looking around, and she didn't see anything but her own discarded clothes. What time was it?

Six o'clock.

He's gone. Throwing back the covers, Connie leapt out of bed. *No, he's not.* She hurried into yesterday's clothes. *He's at the spring. He wouldn't leave—not now. Not after...*

Grabbing soap and a towel, Connie flew out the door and hurried down the path. Doubts, and something not unlike panic, hovered on the fringe of conscious thought, but she refused to give them voice. *He's at the spring.*

But of course he was not. Nor was his pickup in the turn-around, and if those skid marks were any indication, his departure had been a hasty one.

The doubts she had held at bay now closed in like vultures at a kill. They pecked away at her composure and reduced her breathing to rough and shallow pants while she struggled against the urge to cry.

She perched on a rock, knees to chest, chin on knees, arms tightly wrapped around her legs, and stared with dry, burning eyes at the spot where the truck had stood.

So he had left. What did that prove, except that he had to get to work early? Or that he hadn't wanted people in town to see him driving in wearing a satisfied grin and yesterday's rumpled uniform?

Or, of course, it could mean that he regretted having made love to her.

Of all the reasons, why was that the one she believed?

Because, Connie told herself, knowing Jud as she was beginning to, that was the one that rang true. And because, given the length of time he had had to convince himself that city women were not to be trusted and the brevity of time he had had with Connie to learn otherwise, it made sense.

Connie lifted her head, tilting it back to look up at the cloudless, endless expanse of blue overhead. Little by little the lump in her throat dissolved and was swallowed. She breathed deeply and closed her eyes. She had told Jud she loved him. Now she would give him a week to get used to the idea.

It didn't take a week for Jud to convince himself that his night with Connie had been a mistake. He knew it as soon as his tire went flat right in front of the Starbrite Motel at six o'clock the morning after. And, wouldn't you know, there was Elsie herself, disgustingly bright-eyed, sweeping the porch at the crack of dawn.

"Mornin', Jud," she hollered, leaning on the broom and watching with undisguised curiosity as he climbed from the truck. "Did you get caught in the storm?"

Gnashing his teeth, Jud merely waved and hunkered down to assess the damage. Yup, it was a flat, all right. Punctured, most likely. Of all the damn times . . .

Heaving a sigh, he straightened and went to get the jack. The sooner he got the blessed thing changed, the sooner he'd get his half-dressed self off this public street.

He was just loosening the last nut when George Slater, Elsie's husband, ambled up. "See you got yourself a flat tire, Jud."

Jud mentally cursed his luck once again. "Yup."

The nut removed, he pulled the tire off and straightened to heave it into the back of the pickup.

George was eyeing Jud's lack of shirt and his open uniform jacket with interest. "Rough night?" he asked with a gleam of speculation in his eye. "Heard tell they burgled Butler's Peak. Up there, were you?"

"Yup." Jud kept his eyes on the spare, hoisting it into position and wishing George to the devil. As fast as he could pick them up, he positioned the nuts and started tightening.

"That husband o' hers sure didn't hang around very long. Guess he struck out, huh?" George squatted down, shoulder-to-shoulder beside him, jabbing his elbow playfully into Jud's side as he added, "That's quite the little woman up there, I'll bet."

Jud had known George for years, hunted and fished with him, liked him. Right now, though, he wanted nothing so much as to shove the man's three remaining teeth right down his throat.

Lips pressed together lest he say something regrettable, Jud tightened his grip on the wrench and gave the last nut a final vicious twist.

"There," he ground out, "that ought to hold 'er. Excuse me, George."

Shoving just enough to make George totter, he swiftly got to his feet, let down the jack and threw the works into the back of the truck. Hurrying into the cab, he called, "See ya," and was halfway down the block before George regained his balance.

At home he showered, dressed, did morning chores and never stopped cussing. Of all the stupid stunts he'd pulled in his time, spending the night up at the lookout with Constance Martinelli took the prize. He might just as well have taken out an ad in the Mattville Weekly Gazette saying he had the hots for the woman.

It'd be all over town by nine o'clock, tops. Gossip—something new and juicy for a change. Hell, it wasn't himself he was worried about—to the guys in town it'd probably make him some kind of hero—but he hated the thought of Connie's name being bandied about by a bunch of would-be lotharios. She was a fine woman and deserved better.

Lord, what a mess. Thoroughly fed up and disgusted with himself, he stomped off to work.

Paul greeted him cheerfully. "Jud, old buddy, how're you doing?"

Jud merely glowered in passing, but Paul trailed him into his office. "Connie called in a bit ago."

"Oh, yeah?" Jud picked up a stack of letters and riffled through them, wishing Paul to perdition, yet almost aching to hear what Connie had had to say. How had she sounded? She was sure to be upset about the way he'd sneaked off. "She okay?"

"Happy as a lark." Paul punched him playfully in the shoulder. "You old son of a gun." And, whistling, he strode from the room.

Jud stared after him. *Happy as a lark?* What the hell was the meaning of that? How could she be happy? Hadn't she missed him, wondered why and where he'd gone?

Women. Jud dropped into his chair and scowled at the desk. What a mess.

It took several days of soul-searching and veiled, and not-so-veiled, innuendos from the townfolk for Jud to come to the conclusion that in spending the night with Connie he had committed an even greater folly than he had originally thought.

As far as his friends and the good people of Mattville were concerned, he and Connie were now an "item." Going steady. Practically engaged. The whole thing had gotten completely out of hand.

Why, just yesterday, Elsie had stopped Jud in the supermarket and announced in a voice that would have put a town crier to shame that she would be glad to throw Connie a shower just as soon as the date was set. The date!

They expected him to marry Constance Martinelli. Jud tossed forkfuls of hay into a stall, muttering under his breath. Couldn't folks see how ludicrous that was, how wrong he and Connie were for each other?

Well, sir—another forkful sailed through the air—he was done stewing about the problem alone. This concerned Connie as much as it did him, and surely she would want to do something to squelch these wedding rumors on the double. First, though, she'd probably laugh herself silly.

Perversely angered by that notion, he flung the fork down and strode out of the barn. This was Sunday; he'd head up to the Peak and get things settled once and for all. Maybe between them they could come up with some concrete plan of action.

A couple of hours later Jud's heart was drumming loudly in his chest as he climbed the path to the lookout. He figured he must've gotten out of shape from too much desk work lately. With the building in sight, he stopped to catch his breath and saw Connie in shorts and a halter top, wielding what looked like a hoe.

A hoe? Jud walked on slowly, drinking in the sight of her curvy little form. Her pert face was creased with concentration as she hacked at the soil.

Well, I'll be, Jud thought. *She's gardening.* Would the woman never stop amazing him? A lump threatened to clog his throat, and he had to swallow before he could call out.

"Hi there."

At the sound of his voice, Connie started, dropped the hoe and ran toward him with a smile that lit her face like the sun. Launching herself into Jud's arms, she wrapped her arms around his neck, her legs around his middle, and planted her lips on his.

Jud had no choice but to close his arms around her, crush her to him and kiss her like the starving man he was. When at last, breathless, they reluctantly parted, Connie's smile had turned dreamy.

"I knew you would come," she whispered against his mouth. "I'm so glad." And she kissed him again.

All thoughts of town, of showers and of weddings fled as Jud carried Connie into the lookout and lowered her gently onto the bed. In seconds they had shed their clothes and lay entwined on the narrow cot.

"God, I've missed you," Jud muttered into the fragrant hollow at the base of her slender neck, teasing the spot with the tip of his tongue and trailing kisses upward and along the curve of her jaw. His hands were stroking the silky length of her, relishing each peak and valley, glorying in the feel of her. "I missed your sweetness, your warmth...."

Their lips met, clung, devoured each other in a kiss that was all fire and honey. Connie surrendered to the molten waves of delicious sensation that swamped her. She felt secure in the knowledge that Jud loved her now. Why else would he have come? Holding nothing back, she offered herself up to his increasingly intimate explorations.

"I love you, Jud," she whispered, holding him tight, fitting herself against him, so smooth, so right.

This time the words were much easier to take, Jud found, startled by the depth and fierceness of the response they aroused deep within him. He kissed her everywhere, wanting to taste and know her completely.

With something akin to reverence, he explored the velvet skin of her thighs, moving his lips upward until they had

captured the most intimate, the most vulnerable part of her
and gently played there.

"Jud." Connie's hands grasped his head, and her hips
moved. "Oh, Jud, please. *Please*."

With his senses every bit as inflamed as Connie's, Jud
surged upward and kissed her lips while burying himself
deep in the welcoming heat of her body. They found a
rhythm that delighted them both and steadily scaled the
heights of their mutual passion. Clinging together, the
pleasure they shared blinded them to everything else. Faster
they moved and tighter they clung, two souls searching for
a heaven. And then, in one explosive conflagration, their
individual selves ignited, flamed and drifted to earth, the
ashes of their spirits irrevocably mixed.

After days spent worrying, denying, hoping and praying,
they slept.

Waking to the sound of voices out on the path, they shot
out of bed and scrambled for their clothes. "Oh, my gosh,
oh, my gosh," Connie mumbled over and over, hopping
first on one foot, then the other, as she struggled to get into
her shorts. Unable to find the halter she'd worn, she ran to
drag a T-shirt out of a drawer and pull it over her head.

Finger-combing her curls, she finally looked at Jud. He
was perched on the edge of a chair, dressed except for one
boot, which was only half-on and had the missing halter
hanging out of the top of it. His eyes moved from the halter to Connie, lingering on her shirt, raised to meet her gaze.
As if on cue, they both began to laugh.

"Hello!"

Instantly sober, Connie flew to the bed and pulled at the
blankets. "Jud, the door's open, and they're right outside," she hissed, all thumbs in her attempt to hurry.
"You're the ranger. Do something."

He did. On his way out to greet the visitors, he dropped
the halter on the bed and patted her upturned derriere.
"Your shirt's on backward."

Connie snapped upright to give him a stern look, but he was already at the door, calling, "Howdy, folks. Why don't you stay where you are and I'll show you around outside first."

Looking down at herself, Connie saw that Jud was right about the shirt. Listening to his footsteps jogging down the stairs, she hurried to remedy the situation.

By the time he reentered the lookout in the company of a young couple, Connie had regained her poise and was brewing coffee. Since the two mugs were all she had, she poured some for the guests only. They sipped it gratefully, listening with fascination as Jud explained the instruments. Connie excused herself to head for the outhouse.

Ordinarily she would have welcomed the visitors and been proud to tell them about her job up here, but today, right now, she only wished they'd go away and let her enjoy her time with Jud.

He had come, just as she had hoped, known, he would. That had to mean something, at the very least that he cared for her somewhat. Maybe even loved her, though he probably didn't know it yet. He would tell her if he knew it, wouldn't he? Probably not. He'd think it was too soon, not being a man who liked to rush into things.

Connie smiled to herself and peeked out from behind a scraggy pine. He had come, and that was a start.

And the visitors were marching smartly down the path.

Connie hurried back to the lookout and up the stairs. Jud stood at the washstand, rinsing the cups. She ran up and hugged him from behind, pressing her cheek against the solidity of his back. "Hi."

She loosened her grip so that he could turn and rose on tiptoe to meet his mouth. Their kiss was long and loving, thoroughly satisfying. Drawing apart, they shared a smile.

"Thanks for taking care of the visitors for me," Connie said, squeezing his waist. "Talk about rotten timing."

Jud planted a kiss on her nose. Then, unable to stop, he caught her lips and kissed her deeply once again. Connie melted against him, her knees weak and trembling, as desire surged like a hot tide through her veins. She moved her hands down his back, stroked his lean, firmly muscled male buttocks and up again to work her way inside the waistband of his jeans.

Jud groaned, kissed her hard, then not so hard, then not at all. Aching for her though he was, it was time to talk. He reached back and pulled her hands out of his pants, kissing each one before firmly placing them at her side and setting her back a space.

"We need to talk, Connie."

Connie looked up at Jud, saw the by-now-familiar fiery glow in his eyes and the flush of desire on his cheeks and knew that if she chose she could make him forget about talking in seconds. The knowledge filled her with a proud and fierce joy and made it easy for her to say, "Okay."

Smiling up at him, she reached for the mugs he had washed and went to fill them with coffee. "Come and sit down," she said, carrying their drinks to the table.

As soon as they were seated, Jud began. "Elsie is planning to throw you a shower, Helen called to say she's glad I've seen the light, and everybody in the whole damn town is driving me crazy with the looks they give me. And all because I had a flat tire on my way home the other morning."

Connie listened with her mug halfway to her mouth. It stayed there for several blinks of her eyes until she plunked it down on the table with a spurt of laughter.

"You had a flat?" She clapped a hand to her mouth, picturing the scene. "Oh, Jud, that's priceless. Where?"

Jud told her, then watched in mounting exasperation as she laughed even harder. "I didn't come here to get laughed at," he finally groused. "I came to get your help in putting an end to all the foolishness down in Mattville."

Connie sobered immediately. "So *that's* why you came."

Jud saw the hurt in those golden-brown eyes of hers, and
he frowned, bewildered. He reached across the table to cover
her hand with his. "What did I say?"

Connie blinked and looked away. She withdrew her hand
and scooted back on her chair, as if to put as much distance
as possible between them.

"I thought you came because—" She swallowed and
shrugged. Shaking her head, she twisted her lips into a lopsided smile that didn't quite manage to reach her eyes. "I
thought it meant you cared—"

"It did. I do." Jud rounded the table and hunkered down
in front of her. He caught one of her hands and kissed the
knuckles. Holding it between both of his, he said, "I do
care, and I wouldn't want to hurt you for the world. You're
special, Connie, and I—well, I care."

He raised her hand to kiss each finger, turned it to kiss the
palm and finally pressed it against his cheek. "I needed so
much to see you again," he said, emotion roughening his
voice. "And not just because of the rumors."

Moved, knowing by now that to articulate his feelings
even to this extent required almost superhuman effort on
Jud's part, Connie leaned over to touch her mouth to his.
When they drew apart, Jud gave her hand a final squeeze
and rose. He walked to the nearest window and, rubbing the
back of his neck, stared into the distance.

"They're talking weddings down there, did you know
that? Our wedding." He spun to face her, a dark frown
creasing his brow. "Yours and mine. Can you believe it?"

"Well, I—"

"The thing is, not one of those busybodies seems to give
a hot damn what you and I might be after, they're so busy
plotting and planning and minding our business...."

Growing increasingly heavy of heart, Connie watched Jud
turn away and pace the room like a caged animal, all but
snarling a string of protests at the town's meddling ways.
When at last he stopped to stare down at her once more, she

met the fiery indignation of his gaze with all the composure she could muster. Right then, the last thing she wanted was for Jud to see the hurt his outrage was inflicting on her.

"You'd think folks'd have the courtesy to consult us, wouldn't you?" he demanded. "They'd sure as hell find out in a hurry that you, for one, have plans for your life that don't include their little backwater town. Or me," he added more quietly.

Jud jammed both hands into his pants pockets and narrowed his eyes almost to slits. He leaned down and stared at Connie as if he were searching for something in her face.

"Wouldn't they?" he asked softly in a guarded tone.

Connie swallowed against a sudden lump. What was Jud asking? she wondered with a fluttery surge of hope. What was he *really* asking?

She moistened her lips, nervously aware that her very happiness might well hinge on the way she phrased her reply. She had long since decided to stay in Montana, and her mass mailing of résumés had included several addressed to school districts in the state. Thanks to her grandparents, Montana had always had a special place in her heart. If she and Jud should marry—and, God, she prayed they would— then she was sure to have no trouble finding a teaching position nearby.

Jud abruptly straightened and, head high and shoulders set, strode to the shelf by the door and snatched up his hat.

He was leaving! Startled out of her reverie and suddenly aware of how her long, thoughtful silence must have seemed to him, Connie leapt up from her chair.

"Jud, wait. Listen to me."

She rushed over to him and clutched his arm with both hands. Looking up into his carefully blanked face, she struggled for words.

"Jud, how can I answer a question like that," she finally asked, "when I don't really give a tinker's damn what the town thinks or says? It's what you say that's important to me. And it's what you *feel* that I care about.''

She stopped to search his eyes for a clue to his thoughts, but found none. ''What are you saying, Jud? What are you feeling?''

Jud's expression darkened, and the studied neutrality of his gaze turned bleak. He averted his eyes and slammed the hat on his head in a rare show of temper.

''Damned if I know,'' he bit out from between clenched teeth. ''Damned if I know *what* the hell I feel anymore. Look—'' He peeled Connie's unresisting hands off his arm. ''I'll see you, okay?''

Connie's arms fell to her sides, and she took a step backward, away from him. He turned to go, then swung around to face her again. Connie stayed where she was, chin high, gaze steady, betraying by not so much as a quivering muscle the spasms of raw pain that were tearing her heart asunder.

Jud raked her motionless form with eyes gone bright as sapphires from the heat of the battle that raged within his soul. His body jerked as if to move toward her, his lips parted as if for speech, but in the end he only inhaled a sharp breath, spun on his heel and hurried down the lookout stairs as if he were pursued by all the demons of hell.

''Butler's Peak calling Mattville ranger station.''

''Morning, Connie.''

''Hi, Paul. Signing in. Everything's quiet, and pretty darn chilly. Looks like rain—again.''

''Fire season's almost over, kid. Decided where you'll teach yet?''

''Sort of. Helen coming today?''

''Plans to, last I heard. You going to be around?''

''Oh, sure. She won't get here before noon, anyway. I'll be back by then, easy. Rudy and I are taking a hike.''

''Fine and dandy. Watch your step, okay? Over and out.''

Connie replaced the mike, hooked a small backpack containing extra film, several lenses, a thermos and a plastic poncho over her shoulders and hung the camera around her neck. "Okay, Rudy. Let's move it."

They trudged down the stairs and headed off in the direction of the turnaround. Just before they reached it, however, they took a small, barely noticeable path that led them first down and then steeply up toward a wonderful meadow they had discovered about a week ago.

Connie and the dog hiked regularly these days. With the fire danger all but past and visitors down to a mere trickle, it was a way to pass the time that Connie had come to cherish.

Humming, she tramped on, her eyes alternately on the path and on the glorious scenery. Paul's admonition to watch her step, though delivered in a teasing manner, had not been idle chatter. One wrong step could prove fatal in the mountains, a fact of which Connie was very much aware.

She had learned so much this summer, she mused, about nature and weather and coping with adversity. About aloneness, which was good for the soul—and about loneliness, which was not. And about needing both of those conditions in order to learn patience. And tolerance.

Connie stopped walking. Looking around, catching her breath, she wondered how much longer her patience would tolerate Jud Halverson's need for time, how much longer before it snapped and she stormed that log house of his to shake him till his teeth rattled.

Not much longer!

She walked on, diverting herself with a recital of the myriad of exquisite tortures she would inflict on Jud when her patience ran out, or the fire season ended, whichever came first.

Toothpicks inserted beneath each fingernail was one of her tamer daydreams.

But never mind. She hadn't been idle while giving the man another chance to realize he loved and needed her. She'd launched a possible second career. She'd discovered a very enjoyable avocation: nature photography.

So far she'd shot five rolls of excellent subjects—if she might be permitted to brag. Flowers, birds, small animals—nearly all the abundant alpine flora and fauna had been captured on film by Constance Jacobi. She would use her maiden name as a pseudonym, she had decided, thinking that Constance Halverson lacked a certain artistic ring. As she had done so often growing up as an only child, Connie amused herself with fantasies....

...and thanks to my father, Donovan Jacobi, M.D., for the gift of the camera that afforded me the opportunity...

Still too wordy and stilted. Oh, well, there was time yet to worry about the right way to phrase the dedication in the front of her bestselling book of photographs. First the film had to be developed and printed.... Then a horrible thought occurred to her. What if they hadn't turned out?

Nonsense. Connie waved the unworthy doubt aside. How could they not? All it took was a good subject, the turn of a lens and the click of the button.

Connie stopped to wipe her brow and get her bearings. The sun was breaking through the thin layer of clouds. Great for photography. Her pictures were bound to be better with the sunlight adding sharpness and contrast. She squinted ahead, noting that just beyond the stand of pines she would have to follow the fork to the right.

"Rudy."

He had gotten way ahead of her. She must have dawdled while deep in thought. Hiking more briskly, Connie hurried to catch up with the dog. She looked in every direction, straining to distinguish his dark, shiny form from the low shrubs and multisize boulders that dotted the terrain.

"Rudy! Come, bo— Ouch! Oh, no... *Rudy!*"

Connie collapsed in a heap, her right leg firmly and immovably stuck in a narrow crevice, despite her immediate efforts to pull free.

She was trapped—as surely and as painfully as any animal trapped by man. No wonder she had always hated the idea; it was a terrible, frightening experience. Where was Rudy! *"Rudeee... Oh, God, I'm going to die!"*

The thought had barely formed and the sob had not yet escaped when Connie squelched both. *I will not panic.* She arranged her free leg in as comfortable a position as she could, took a deep breath and squeezed her eyes tightly shut. *Think,* she exhorted herself. Stay calm and...

"Yipes!" Something cold and wet touched her face; Connie's eyes flew open, and her heart skipped a half-dozen beats and then pounded like a jackhammer run amok. "What on earth—Rudy!" Throwing both arms around the Doberman's neck, Connie gave herself up to a thorough tongue-licking.

"Am I glad to see you, boy... Where did you get to? I'm in trouble here, I think. Actually, I'm sure of it. Rudy, I need your help, so listen."

She was babbling. Connie closed her mouth and took a deep breath. *I will not panic.* "I'm stuck here. See?"

She moved her body so that Rudy could fully appreciate the severity of their circumstances, but he seemed not to care at all. He was off like a streak, never once looking back at his hurt and stricken mistress.

Nine

"Yoo-hoo, Connie. You home?"

Helen's voice cast a fine echo, but elicited no response. She turned to Jud, who had lagged behind, wishing he'd had the presence of mind to dream up some other destination when approached by Helen down at the ranger station. On hearing that he was headed for Butler's Peak, she had given a delighted laugh and announced, "Wonderful—now I can hitch a ride with you."

And here they were.

"Jud." Helen was frowning at him. "I said, I guess she's not back yet."

Jud gave an absent nod. "Doesn't look like it."

He was thinking that it might be a good idea to walk out a ways and intercept Connie. That would give them at least a little privacy to say a few words without Helen's eagle eye watching their every move.

Connie was bound to be furious with him for walking out on her again the other Sunday. Not that he blamed her; he'd been plenty riled with himself, too. But just the same, he wouldn't appreciate an audience when he struggled with the explanation he knew he'd have to come up with.

"Jud Halverson, are you deaf?" Helen had gone ahead upstairs and inside and was standing in the doorway waving a red-and-white can of soup at him. "I said, I'm going to fix lunch. D'you like chicken noodle?"

"That's fine." Jud waved a hand and nodded. "Think I'll nose around a bit, see if I run into Connie."

Helen's answering grin was knowing. "Sure, why don't you do that?"

Jud set out on the trail that passed the outhouse and meandered through a meadow in the direction of Widow's Peak, an outcropping of rocks so named for no reason Jud knew of. He had no idea if Connie had chosen this way, but decided to walk for a bit and see.

Deep in thought, he followed the rapidly dwindling trail, but kept a sharp eye out for any movement or flash of color that could be Connie or the dog. The longer he walked, the more his eyes narrowed, and after some fifteen minutes he was scowling mightily. Where the hell were they, and what in tarnation was the woman thinking of, wandering this far afield. She was a novice in tackling these hills, dammit, but he'd have bet his pension she fancied herself a seasoned mountaineer.

Which was exactly the kind of rationale she applied to everything, including their relationship. Once her enthusiasm was sparked, she seemed blind to any and all pitfalls and blithely forged ahead. He, himself, on the other hand—

Jud's brooding thoughts abruptly stopped as Rudy's sleek form bounded into his field of vision. Tongue flopping, the dog ran as if a swarm of hornets were on his tail.

Jud strained to spot Connie, but she was not yet in sight.

"Whoa, boy." He laughed, fending off the dog's almost-frantic greeting. Rudy was bouncing up against Jud's chest, barking in a way that would have alarmed anyone not familiar with his gentle nature. He was intimidating in his agitation, nipping at Jud's hands as if to take hold of them, running up the path and back again and again.

"What's the matter, Rudy? Where's Connie?" Jud hunkered down, took hold of the dog's head and looked him in the eye. "Where's Connie, boy?"

Rudy struggled to be free, ready to run back the way he had come, but Jud knew the dog needed water. And Jud needed to tell Helen that it looked as if Connie was in trouble.

"Come, boy," he said to the reluctant animal. "Come take a drink, and then we'll find her."

We *will* find her, he vowed to himself.

He was still clinging to that conviction some forty-five minutes later, but only barely. It seemed he had jogged behind the dog forever, and still there was no sign of Connie. Only his faith in Rudy's loyalty to his mistress, his obvious love for her, kept Jud following in the canine footsteps. The dog knew where he was going. Jud had to believe that.

She was okay, she had to be. How could he lose her before he had really found her? Before he'd had the chance to explain—

"She'll Be Coming Round the Mountain" was being sung by a familiar, if somewhat shaky, voice. Connie. Happiness and relief mingled in a flood of emotion that washed the starch right out of him. He stopped, blinking against a sudden blurring of his vision, as Rudy barreled into the small form huddled on the ground just a little way up the trail.

"Rudy!" Connie threw her arms around the dog's neck, and her voice grew muffled as she pressed her face against his shiny coat. "I'm so glad you came back."

"And he brought me along," Jud announced, joining them, as close to crying as he'd ever been in his adult life.

Connie's head snapped up. Her eyes were as bright as agates beneath a sheen of unshed tears as she stared at him.

"Jud." Her voice cracked, and her sweet face crumpled, along with her staunch courage. "Oh, Jud."

Jud was on his knees and had Connie clasped against his chest before the last sigh of his name had faded. His mouth traced every part of her face and settled briefly, scorchingly, on her lips. "Oh, God, Connie. I've been out of my mind."

His lips claimed hers again, then rained kisses along the curve of her jaw. "I thought I'd lost you, and I couldn't stand it. Never do this again, do you hear me? Never again..."

Connie was laughing and crying all at once. She gave herself up to Jud's kisses and savored every desperate word he uttered.

Jud was here. For the moment, she needed nothing more.

Ruthlessly tamping down the desperation that urged him to keep Connie crushed against his heart, Jud gradually relaxed the pressure of his arms. He needed to know how seriously she was hurt. He needed to know how to help her. His roaming hands slid along Connie's arms to cup her shoulders, and, with a final kiss on the perky tip of her nose, he settled back on his heels.

"Let's get you out of this mess as quickly as possible," he murmured, his voice husky with emotion. He pointed at the backpack on the ground next to Connie. "You got anything in there that could be of help? Like an ax?"

Connie shook her head. "Just a thermos of water, my camera and some lenses. Dumb, huh?"

"No, of course not." Jud gave her shoulder a reassuring squeeze before releasing her to shift his attention to the trapped leg. "You weren't planning to chop wood, after all. I only asked because it'd surely be a handy tool for getting you loose from this hole in the ground. Helen's waiting lunch and told me to hurry. You know how testy that woman gets when she's crossed...."

While Jud joked about Helen, he poked and prodded to see what was what. The edges of the crevice were jagged and sharp, and Connie's leg was trapped clear up to the knee. He could only hope that the sturdy denim of her jeans and the high-topped hiking boots she wore had prevented any really deep cuts in her foot and leg.

"Can you move at all?" he asked, leaning down and reaching into the narrow, trenchlike crevice that gripped the sides of Connie's leg like a vise. He felt for her booted foot and, reaching down more deeply, fumbled for a hold on its reinforced toe. With utmost care he tried to jog the foot just a little.

"Do you feel this? Does it hurt?"

"No, everything's numb." Connie clutched at Jud's back for balance and squeezed her eyes shut against a resurgence of tears. "I *hate* feeling so damned helpless," she wailed. "Tell me what to do, Jud, *please*."

"Hush now." Jud let go of Connie's foot and straightened. "You just take it easy and let *me* do the work."

He pulled a hunting knife from its sheath on his belt. His free hand briefly touched Connie's cheek, and his thumb wiped away a wayward tear. "It'll be fine, I promise," he murmured, praying the words would prove to be as prophetic as they were meant to be reassuring. "Just get as comfortable as you can while I see if I can't widen this trench a bit. Okay?"

Connie nodded, ashamed of her weakness, and managed a lipsided smile. "Okay."

"That's my girl." Jud's answering smile was replaced by a look of grim resolve as he bent to the task of setting her free. He chipped at the rocky dirt with controlled force while Connie contented herself with watching the ripple of muscles beneath his red-and-black checked shirt and remembering the hard, marble-smooth feel of them. *That's my girl,* she thought dreamily. Had he meant that?

A grunt of exertion followed by a stifled curse snapped Connie out of her reverie in time to see a sizable chunk of rock-hard earth splinter and crumble into the crevice. She immediately tried to wiggle her leg, planting both hands on the ground behind her hips for leverage and pulled with all her might.

"It's no good," she panted on a dry sob of frustration and pain, plopping onto her back. "I'm still stuck."

"Relax a minute, honey." Jud's voice was like graveled velvet. He was shoulder-deep in the crevasse now, hacking and twisting and tunneling with his knife. Progress was slow, and perspiration beaded his forehead, running in rivulets into his eyes and down his ruddy cheeks.

Seeing Jud blink against the salty sting of it, Connie straightened from her reclining position, unknotted a small cotton kerchief from around her neck and, like a nurse in an operating room, dabbed with it at the moisture.

"Are you making any progress at all in there?" she asked.

"Think so." Jud grunted with the exertion, twisting and pushing his knife in an effort to loosen or shift the stubborn rock next to Connie's ankle. At last it gave, and Connie felt an immediate lessening of pressure against her limb.

She wiggled, and this time she could move it a little. "You did it!"

She prepared to pull again, but Jud laid a steadying hand on her knee. "Stay still. Let me clear some more space alongside your calf in there," he panted, resuming his labors with relentless care and concentration, his free hand still resting on Connie's thigh.

She covered it with both of her hands, her heart expanding until it filled her chest and stole her breath. How careful he was not to hurt her further, she marveled. How patiently he labored on her behalf. His concern just had to be born of love. Surely his coming today meant . . .

Connie had thought once before that his coming to the lookout meant more than it did. This time there would be no jumping to conclusions. And yet . . .

Jud tightened his grip on her leg almost painfully, then relaxed as another chunk disintegrated and Connie's leg no longer felt clamped in place.

"Jud, I'm loose." She hugged his arm. "I can move my leg."

With her relief and excitement, adrenaline coursed through her veins. Connie felt able to leap to her feet and dance a jig.

Jud straightened, chest heaving, and tossed the knife aside. As if he'd read her mind, he shook his head and said, "Just stay put now, honey, and let me do the rest of it. You're loose, but you're not out of the woods yet."

He scrambled around and in front of Connie, straddling the crevice. Working his hands into the trench on either side of her trapped leg until he cupped her foot, he slowly lifted and tugged and raised the limb with utmost care.

"Does this hurt?" he asked, breathless from the renewed effort. "This?"

"A bit," Connie gasped, biting her lip to stifle a groan. "But . . . Oh! *Ouch!*"

A jolt of pain brought her to a sitting position, and then she collapsed onto her back as the leg was pulled free. "Thank God," she murmured, squeezing her burning eyes shut.

Jud was at her side and gathering her up in an instant. "It's over, sweetheart. You're fine," he crooned.

Secure in Jud's arms, Connie gave in to a moment of weakness. She had been alone for nearly three hours, trapped in that infernal crack in the earth. "I was so scared."

It felt good to admit it. She hid her face against Jud's chest and wrapped her arms around his middle.

"You were brave," he whispered into the crown of her hair. She could feel his lips moving as he spoke the words, stroking her scalp, his breath a warm and sensuous caress.

"I prayed you'd come," Connie said into his shirt, pressing kisses against the sweat-dampened fabric and breathing deeply of his scent. "I needed you so much."

"Oh, Connie." Jud tunneled a hand into the sun-streaked riot of her curls and tilted her head. His lips claimed hers with hungry authority, his tongue the hunter, hers the willing prey.

Connie's moan was one of pleasure, but Jud immediately gentled his caress. He cupped her cheek, his thumb stroking her jaw. He loved and savored her mouth with bone-melting tenderness, striving to convey in ways other than words the things she was making him feel.

Connie felt cherished, adored and more desirable than she would ever have thought it possible to feel. Clutching his shoulders, she gave herself up to the wondrous sensations rippling through her like currents of electricity.

All too soon, Jud pulled away. He rocked back on his heels and framed her face with hands that shook.

"Woman," he rasped, "as much as I'd delight in kissing you forever, I'd best check the damage now and get you home."

Connie smiled through the rosy haze that enveloped her. She lay back and submitted to Jud's probing touches without protest. The sooner they were on their way, the sooner they could be alone together in much more congenial surroundings.

Jud gripped the already-torn fabric of Connie's jeans and ripped it to midthigh. His breath caught at the sight of the long gash that extended from the top of her boot to the side of her knee. Blood oozed from it thickly, its crimson brilliance obscene against the fairness of her skin. Careful not to betray his dismay, Jud pulled a clean handkerchief from his pocket and gently dabbed at the wound.

Thank God for the wonderful state of this woman's health, he thought, noting that most of the blood was already forming a coagulated crust across the gash. And thank God no major vein had been struck. As it was, some neat stitching and the passage of time would leave the leg marred by only the faintest of scars.

Somewhat reassured, Jud next unlaced Connie's boot and removed both it and the thick woolen sock she wore inside. Her ankle was beginning to discolor, but looked otherwise normal.

"Wiggle your toes," he commanded softly. "But easy, careful now."

Connie did as he asked. "What do you think?"

Jud's hands, cradling her foot and rotating it to test the joint, were sure and gentle. "I think that nothing is broken and that you're one very lucky young woman. You'll need some stitches, but other than that..."

He set her foot down gently and, still on his knees, bent forward to smile at her. "...I think you'll be just fine, Mrs. Martinelli."

Connie stroked Jud's face, mixing dust with the perspiration there. "Thank you for coming, today of all days. I don't know what I would've done..."

"Hush now. It's over."

Their gazes clung, and Jud saw a world of promise reflected in the hazel depths of hers. A wave of some strange and nameless emotion threatened to set his thoughts adrift on an uncharted course that scared him to death. He jerked himself back.

"Time to go," he said, his voice clipped now. Immediately regretting the words and the brusque tone in which they had been uttered, he laid both of Connie's hands in her lap without a word and got to his feet. Bending, he handed her the sock to put on, picked up the boot and tied its laces to his belt. Then he lifted Connie into his arms and straightened. Holding her clasped tightly against his chest, he started the long walk home with Rudy at his side.

Jud held Connie like that all the way back to the lookout, careful not to jostle her, mindful that, though nothing seemed to be broken, her ankle was swelling and obviously causing her discomfort. Connie made no complaint, but her silence told its own story.

Her small form was no burden; on the contrary, she seemed to weigh almost nothing at all. Such a bitty thing, he marveled, as he so often had, but packed chock-full of character. She was quite a woman. *So how come you don't tell her so? Ask her to stay? Tell her you care?*

Jud trudged on doggedly, the answers to those questions as elusive as ever.

All too soon, as far as Connie was concerned, the lookout came into view. She had enjoyed the ride, securely clasped against Jud's broad chest, feeling his warmth, his seemingly boundless strength. He walked with purpose, sure and straight, not only on this mountain path, but on life's path, as well. He was a man who knew himself and consequently could be true to himself. He was a man who, once committed to loving a woman, would be forever true to her. This Connie knew with unshakable certainty.

She tightened her grip on Jud's neck and nuzzled the warmly pulsing hollow at the base of his throat. She wanted to be that woman. His woman. How could she make him see that he wanted that, too?

Helen was running toward them, her anxiety evident in the uncoordinated movements of her body. She was hop-skipping in an effort to protect her sandaled feet from the worst of the rocks and pebbles; and her arms were flailing like windmills. She was shouting before she could possibly be heard.

"...been nearly out of my mind. What took you so long? How bad is she?" could finally be deciphered as she came closer. She stopped in front of Jud and his burden and enfolded them both in her arms.

"God, I'm glad to see you guys. It's been hours since you took off after her, Jud. What happened out there? What did she do to herself?"

"What's this 'she' stuff?" Connie complained. "I hurt my leg, but there isn't a thing wrong with my ears or my voice. Jud says I'll be fine."

"Well, hallelujah." Helen released her hold on them and stepped back to glare at her injured friend. "I'd never have forgiven you if you'd seriously hurt yourself. Why couldn't you just stay put? You knew I was coming."

They were on their way up the stairs, Helen nattering as she trailed behind them.

Connie threw her an exasperated look over Jud's shoulder. "Will you stop fussing, Helen? I'm fine."

"We'll let Doc Landon have the final word on that," Jud said.

"Not before lunch." Helen bustled ahead to hold the door. "Good thing I heated chicken soup. It's supposed to have healing qualities."

Jud lowered a very skeptical Connie onto the bunk. "I thought that was for colds," she murmured into his ear.

He chuckled and kissed the tip of her nose. "I'm glad your injuries are relatively light—you have the makings of a very nasty patient, Mrs. Martinelli."

Connie ate lunch on the bed, her protests having been jointly overridden. Afterward, Helen cleaned up the dishes while Jud went to refill the buckets for future use and Connie opened the mail Helen had brought.

There were three more replies to her résumés, two of them negative, the other a very lucrative offer from a private school in New York City. At one time Connie would have jumped at such a choice position, but now she laid it aside without giving it a second thought. She had already been to see the superintendent in nearby Stevensville and was confident she would find employment in the grade school there.

"Any tempting offers?" Helen queried, giving the table a final desultory swipe with the dishcloth. "That Hawthorne Academy sounds like it'd be right up your alley." She stopped pretending to wipe and sent Connie a wide-eyed, innocent look. "Or have you changed your mind about that?"

Conne shrugged, hesitant to confide in Helen, but instantly tossed her reservations to the wind. "Yes, I have," she said, almost defiantly. "I'm staying right here in Montana."

"Hal-le-lu-jah! I knew that man would see sense!" Helen tossed the dishrag aside and spun in a circle like a top, careening to a stop almost as soon as she'd begun. "When did he propose? Today?" she demanded to know.

"No!" Aghast at Helen's assumption even as she wished it were true, Connie scooted to the edge of the bed to get up. "Helen, he hasn't— *Ouch!*" As soon as she put weight on her foot, she fell back down in pain.

"Connie." Helen rushed over and gripped her shoulders. "Don't try to stand, you cabbagehead. Jud—"

"Will have your hide, young lady," the man in question cut in sharply, entering with his load of water. "Sit."

"I'm sitting, I'm sitting," Connie groused, screwing her eyes up at him. "Gee, you're bossy."

"You don't know the half of it. Try standing again and see what happens." He put the buckets in their place beneath the washstand and turned toward the bunk.

"Threats—so typical of the male of the species." Connie pulled a face. "You Tarzan, me—"

"In trouble, is what you are." Jud's sparkling eyes belied the stern tone of voice he affected. He bent and seemingly without effort, swung her up into his arms.

Helen pressed both hands to her heart and looked from one to the other. "Ah," she sighed, "ain't love grand?"

Shaking his head, Jud headed for the door. "If you two ladies—and I use the term with distinct reservations—if you're through being cute, I say we get out of here. Bring her purse, will you, Helen?"

Tucked into bed in Paul and Helen's guest room at last, Connie lay on her back and drowsily contemplated the events of the day. What a day!

The visit with the doctor had been relatively brief but anything but pleasant. He had cleaned, stitched and bound the gash that nauseated more than pained her, and she had been characteristically squeamish and complaining throughout the entire procedure. Then Doc Langdon had taped her ankle, which had sustained a pulled ligament, and, as a final act of torture, had administered a tetanus shot before sending her home with a small supply of painkillers and the admonition to quit hiking for a spell.

On Jud's insistence, Connie had agreed to let Helen pamper her, but she was determined to return to her lookout duties just as soon as possible. Her days on Butler's Peak were nearing their end, and she wanted to make the most of her remaining time there.

Strange, she mused now, how much she'd grown to love it on her mountaintop. She had arrived with such distorted expectations, imagining in spite of what the training had taught her that the summer would be a sabbatical of sorts.

Well, it hadn't been that, but she had learned so much. After the turmoil of her divorce, she had finally come full circle back to herself. She had completed her education and prepared for a career. And by virtue of this summer job she had, bit by bit, found and shaped all the fragments of her character into a new and whole person. A person who could love and respect herself, a person able to love a man like Raymond Judson Halverson.

Jud. So much of him was tied up in the way she felt about the lookout. Such memories . . . And she wondered . . . No, she thought, shifting restlessly on the guest-room bed, she *feared* that instead of being happy ones, those memories of Jud were destined to be bittersweet. Ah, Jud . . .

His name blended sweetly into the dreams that followed.

"Connie? Connie, are you awake?"

Helen's voice, along with some loud knocking on the door, was rudely tearing Connie out of Jud's loving arms just when he . . .

"Connie?"

Connie opened one eye, willing Jud's image to stay, willing the voice to fade away. "What?"

Helen was smiling down at her. "Telephone, Your Ladyship."

"At this hour?" The other eye open, Connie struggled to sit up, then blinked when Helen pulled the drapes and let the sunshine in.

"This hour, as you put it, is nine o'clock. Decent folk are up—but in this case it happens to be Vincent on the phone."

"Vincent?" Connie gingerly lowered her feet to the floor and stood, groaning. "What does he want?"

Helen handed Connie a robe and the cane they had rented, saying in her most proper tone, "Since he and I are not on speaking terms, naturally I didn't ask. Nor did he volunteer that morsel of information. Are you coming?" She waited at the door. "It *is* long-distance."

"Let him wait," Connie muttered, thinking that Vincent Martinelli and his schemes were the last thing she wanted to have to deal with this morning. Her leg hurt, and her body wanted to get back to that dream.

She hobbled toward the door.

"How is your leg?" Helen asked, watching.

"Just great," Connie snapped, taking her frustration out on the only available person.

"Testy, aren't we?" Helen tossed her head and stalked off. "You can take the call in the den."

Connie was instantly contrite. She hated hurting people's feelings, especially nice, loving people like Helen, without whom she would often have been lost. She would definitely have to apologize just as soon as she got Vincent off the phone.

"Hello." Connie's tone was cold, and she steeled her sensibilities against whatever outrageous proposition he was going to insult them with this time.

"Prudence has had a stroke and is asking for you."

Connie nearly dropped the phone. *This* she hadn't expected. "What? A stroke? Good God, Vincent, I can't—"

Taking a deep breath, Connie struggled to come to grips with what she'd heard. It couldn't be true, she railed, not Prudence. She'd always been so strong, had seemed so indestructible. She swallowed the tears that threatened to spill.

"Connie?"

"I'm here. How, uh...how bad is she?"

"Pretty bad. How soon can you get here?"

"Get there? I—" She broke off. Suspicion was a viper rearing its head. Vincent sounded awfully chipper for someone whose only close and living relative was at death's door. "Vincent, are you sure this is on the level?"

"Well." The word held galaxies of disillusionment and pain. "Now I certainly know just how low you think I am, don't I, Constance?"

Connie winced, chagrined. Surely even Vincent wouldn't stoop to uttering so cruel a lie just to get his way. Would he?

"I'm sorry I disturbed you," he was saying, his voice brittle. "I'll try my best to make Grandmother understand that—"

"Wait. Please. Vincent, I'm sorry." Connie closed her eyes and swallowed. "I'll come. Of course I'll come if she wants me there. It's just that I, well, I injured my leg, you see, and—"

"Can you walk at all?"

"Well, I have a cane and—"

"Good," Vincent said, sounding relieved. Was there smugness in his voice, too?

"A wheelchair and a first-class ticket will be waiting for you at the airport in Missoula," Vincent went on to inform her, saying that she'd be flying to Denver and from there nonstop to LaGuardia, where she would be met. He sounded crisp and businesslike and altogether too much like a man who expected no protest when he ended by saying he would see her the following night.

He broke the connection before Connie could voice a protest, and she slowly lowered the receiver away from her ear. For a long moment she frowned at it as if at some alien object. Her head was spinning. She felt as if she'd been caught in a storm of events that was sweeping her along like a mindless bit of dust.

Prudence ill. What had happened?

Connie chewed at her bottom lip, unaware that the telephone receiver dropped onto its cradle from fingers as numb as the rest of her body.

Not only ill, but dying, Vincent had said. It seemed impossible. She was only…what? Seventy? Not so young. But, then again, not so old. And until now so very vital.

"She can't be dying."

"Who?"

Connie's jerked toward the sound. Jud was leaning against the door frame, brows shaped into questioning arches, eyes bright with sympathetic warmth.

"Oh, Jud." She made to move toward him, needing his strength, but Jud closed the space between them in two long strides. His arms closed around her slender form to hold her tight. He pressed first his lips, then his cheek, against the top of her head.

"What is it, sweetheart?"

"It's Prudence." Connie kept her face buried against the front of his shirt, inhaling the familiar scent of him, loving the feel of him. "My ex-husband's grandmother."

She lifted her head and pulled back so that she could look at Jud. "She's very dear to me, Jud, as dear as if she were my own relation instead of his. She's had a stroke."

Jud's brows lowered along with his voice. "Who was that on the phone?"

Connie forced back the tears that welled up again so that she could meet his gaze with a level one of her own. "It was Vincent. He wants me to come."

"I see." Hands gripping her shoulders like a vise, Jud lowered his face to within inches of hers. All expression was gone from eyes that only an instant before had glowed so warmly. "Are you planning to do what he asks this time?"

Connie reached up and laid a hand along his cheek. "Jud," she beseeched, willing him to understand, "don't you see, I have to? It's not for Vincent, it's for Prudence. She's been a friend, and more than that, to me. Jud, he says she may not live. She's asking for me."

For several long heartbeats their gazes locked. Jud's eyes were as clear and as fathomless as a glacier lake. Connie shivered beneath their icy glare.

"Jud, what are you thinking?" she asked, a sense of foreboding creeping into her veins like an evil fog. "Say something."

"What are you planning to do about your dog?"

"What?" She was thrown off balance by the question, which was voiced as casually as if they were two strangers who were discussing the weather. Connie stared at Jud. It took a few moments before she realized that he had withdrawn from her the way he always did when confronted with emotions he wasn't ready to handle. Did he think she was leaving for good?

She lifted her other hand, thus framing his face and drawing his head down until she could lay her lips against his in the sweetest of kisses.

"I'll be back in just a few days," she whispered against his passive mouth. "Would you keep Rudy for me? He loves you—just as I do."

Jud closed his eyes. He didn't return Connie's kiss, but neither did he pull away. When at last Connie did, he reached up and pulled her hands from his face. Keeping them clasped in his own, he stared down at them.

"I'll take care of him," he finally said. Releasing her, he stepped back and touched the brim of his hat. "You take care, too."

He was out the door before Connie's cry of protest could leave her suddenly parched and aching throat. Tears burned like acid in her eyes as she stared on the spot where only seconds before Jud had stood.

Ten

———

The sun's fiery mass was as yet hidden behind the Rocky Mountains, but its preceding rays reached out to bathe the sky in brilliant reds and golds. It promised to be a fine day.

Jud, negotiating the familiar road winding its way up to Butler's Peak, was oblivious to the beauty around him. He stared straight ahead, his mood swinging between misery and some undefined anger. On the seat next to him, ears drooping, Rudy was the picture of dejection.

Connie had been gone six days now, and even though she'd called him twice and at first must actually have intended to come back, Jud now knew without a doubt that she no longer had any such intention.

She had phoned Paul yesterday. Not him—Jud—but Paul. She'd told him to go ahead and pack up her stuff. To close the lookout. She'd said she couldn't be sure when she'd be returning, but likely not soon enough to work the lookout anymore.

Jud felt a fierce stab of pain and quickly masked it with rage. What a little coward she was turning out to be, just when he had started to think she could handle anything life dished out. Hiding behind an old woman's sickbed, afraid to face either Paul or him and admit what he'd known to be true all along. That she'd had her fill of wilderness and woodsmen. That she wouldn't be back. Ever.

He'd said as much to Paul yesterday, and the fool had laughed at him. Called him a doubting Thomas, teased him about having second thoughts now that it looked as if he and Connie might tie the knot.

Fool. Jud hadn't dignified his ravings with an answer. *Tie the knot.*

Jud snorted, stoking the anger he knew to be unreasonable but unable to do otherwise. As if someone like her would seriously consider marrying the likes of him, he thought bitterly, dredging up all the prejudices he'd ever harbored against her. Hadn't he known she wouldn't last, hadn't he said so all along? And wasn't he glad now that he'd been right?

Jud pressed his lips together and clenched his teeth to keep a scornful laugh from escaping. He slowed to take a tricky curve while contemplating his distinct lack of joy at being right. If the truth were known, right now he hated being right every bit as much as he hated thinking of Connie back in that city. Back among the things he would never be able to offer her here. Back with that fancy husband . . .

Had the man kissed her yet, seduced her yet? Had he felt, as Jud had, the heat of her response, heard her mindless words of passion?

"I almost believed her, boy," Jud said to Rudy, his tone a grating rasp even to his own ears. "I almost believed her when she said she didn't love him, would never want him again."

They had reached the turnaround. Jud slammed the gear into park and set the hand brake without conscious thought. He stared straight ahead, sightless, all his attention focused inward. And he saw Connie in a hundred moods of laughter, temper, joy and...love. Her eyes alight with invitation, her lips, silky, moist and begging to be kissed, moving now in speech. Whispering, "I love you, Jud—"

With an oath so explosive that it reduced poor Rudy to a quivering heap near the passenger door, Jud slammed out of the pickup and all but ran up the path to the lookout.

Rudy leapt out of the open window and ran after him, but hung well back from the scowling man he'd been left with.

You're a fool, Jud Halverson, Jud was telling himself harshly. He was a fool for believing her, and an even greater fool for offering to pack her gear. *Offering, hell,* he jeered. *You insisted, you sap.*

And so he had. Jud slowed his pace. He would do it and be done with her.

Belatedly he remembered Rudy and stopped walking altogether. He turned and looked back. As soon as he did, the dog—some fifteen feet behind him—sat down and eyed him warily.

Remorse chased away any lingering remnants of Jud's ire. Whatever else he might do in a fit of temper, mistreating an animal was not among the choices.

"Come, boy," he called, gentling his tone and slapping a hand against his thigh in a beckoning gesture. "Come, Rudy."

Very slowly, his belly almost dragging along the ground in a submissive crouch, Rudy approached. Jud watched with an ache in his heart, and when at last the dog lay prone in front of him he reached down to gently stroke the sleek head.

"You miss her, don't you, boy?" Jud murmured, and lowered himself to his knees. He wrapped both arms around the cowering dog and lifted him against his chest. Pressing his cheek against Rudy's satiny muzzle, he crooned, "I know...I know..." mindless of anything but the misery the two of them shared.

The deserted lookout was dismal in spite of Connie's hodgepodge of colorful belongings. Jud forced himself to enter, then stood for a long time just looking at everything and feeling like an intruder.

Why had he come? And how was he ever going to get through this when every book, every colorful cushion, every plant, reminded him of the woman he was trying so hard to blot from his mind.

There were those curtains— God, how he'd raged over those silly bits of fabric. But she'd been right, he noted now. They did make the place seem homier.

The thought barely completed, Jud spun on his heel and clattered down the stairs. He unlocked the storeroom, yanked out some boxes and, his face muscles tight and sore from the strain of keeping any outward expression of his tortured thoughts from showing, commenced packing up Constance Martinelli's belongings.

He worked without letup until he was done. Even when he was stuffing her clothes into a suitcase, holding those fluffy bits of underwear and the halter that had once been carelessly flung aside in their haste to feel each other's bodies... Even then Jud didn't slow his furious pace.

His jaw set rigidly, he didn't permit his hands to linger on any one item or his thoughts to stray from the task of counting to one hundred over and over again.

"Jud." Helen switched off the vacuum cleaner. "I didn't hear you come in. All done at the Peak?"

"I put her stuff in the shed, like you wanted."

"Great, thanks." Helen led the way into the kitchen, removing a red bandanna from her head as she went. "Coffee?"

After lifting two mugs off the hooks underneath one of the cupboards, she reached for the coffeepot. About to pour, she glanced at Jud, who still had not said a word. Setting the pot down again, she frowned at him. "What's wrong?"

He was leaning against the doorjamb, arms folded, and studying Helen as if he were seeing her for the first time. She was Connie's friend more than his, he thought. Was she in on this charade?

"Heard from Connie yet today?"

Helen's frown deepened. She looked bewildered as she shook her head. "No, not yet. Jud, what's going on? Why are you looking at me like that?"

"Like what?"

"Like . . . like you're mad at me or something."

Jud pushed away from the door. His eyes held hers captive as he stalked toward her. "Did she tell you she wasn't coming back here?" he demanded harshly. "Did she?"

"What?" Helen cried, clearly fed up with his strange behavior. "Jud, what the devil are you talking about?"

"I'm talking about your friend. I'm talking about her getting a phone call and hightailing it back to the city. About her leaving us to cope with the lookout, leaving us to do the job she was hired to do for the season, that's what I'm talking about."

Helen eyed him as she might have a lunatic. "You're crazy, Jud," she announced flatly. "You're talking yourself into a state, and why? The fire season is over, it's been raining every day but this one since she left, and she *is* coming back."

Jud stood unmoving, glaring at Helen even when she rounded the kitchen counter to confront him face-to-face.

"Jud, what on earth's gotten into you all of a sudden? For Pete's sake, talk to me. How can you think she's gone for good when you asked her to marry you and she—"

"I *what*?" Jud gripped Helen's shoulders tightly. "What did you just say?"

Helen's mouth dropped open in surprise. She struggled to loosen his grip, and when she didn't succeed she delivered a well-aimed kick to his shin. "Let go of me, you idiot!" she shouted. "I've had it with you."

Jud released her immediately, horrified at his caveman tactics and his loss of control. "I"m sorry, Helen. Please..." He put a shaky hand over his eyes and inhaled deeply. "I don't know what I'm doing anymore."

Dropping his hand, he met her look of concern and felt even worse. "I'm sorry..."

"Don't, Jud." Helen came to stand beside him. She reached out to touch his arm, but he pulled away. She clasped her hands instead and spoke softly. "Jud, I don't understand what's going on here. The day of the accident Connie told me she was staying in Montana for good. You proposed to her, remember?"

Jud shook his head, frowning. "I didn't. What are you saying?"

"I'm saying—no, wait. Let's back up a minute." Helen turned away from Jud to return to her position behind the kitchen counter. "Did you or did you not propose marriage to Connie?"

Jud's frown grew fierce. "I did not. Never." Thank God, he added inwardly, for wouldn't he look an even bigger fool now?

"But she said she was staying. I assumed—"

"You assumed wrong, Helen. And you probably heard wrong, too. Give me one good reason why she'd want to stay."

"I'll give you two." Helen's tone brooked no contradiction. "One, she likes it here. And, two, she loves you."

Jud's short laugh was bitter. "So she said."

"She does, Jud...but tell me this...." Helen's voice grew soft. "What is it you feel for her?"

Jud felt the blood drain from his face and pool icily in his gut. Unable to tear his gaze away from Helen's challenging one, he struggled to form a reply. He searched his brain and he searched his heart, but the one was blank and the other was an aching void.

Without a word, he turned and stalked from the room.

Helen stared after him, one hand half-raised as if to beckon him back. Slowly she lowered it and reached for the coffeepot. Leaning a hip against the counter, she poured some of the steaming black brew into one of the mugs. The telephone shrilled. She set the mug down and picked up the receiver.

"Hello."

"Helen, it's me," Connie said. She leaned back in the small gilded chair in front of an equally ornate vanity table and wished she were back on Butler's Peak. "You got a minute?"

"A minute," Helen exclaimed. "I've got as long as it takes to get to the bottom of this."

Connie held the receiver away from her ear and eyed it for a moment. What had gotten Helen so bent out of shape? "To the bottom of what? Helen, you're not making sense."

"Why should I be the only one who does? You have no idea of the craziness that's going on around here. Tell me one thing, though, before we go any further. Are you or are you not coming back here?"

"What?"

"Just answer yes or no."

"Yes! Of course. I said I would. Helen, what's going on?"

"I'm not sure, but it ain't good, whatever it is. Jud's convinced himself you're staying in New York. He just marched out of here."

"I see." Connie wasn't surprised. She'd felt his emotional withdrawal the day of Vincent's phone call, and she'd sensed it more strongly the two times she had called Jud from New York City. He'd been polite, even cordial, but there had been no warmth, no spark of interest, that she could discern. Now, having had her instincts proved correct, she felt curiously unaffected. Almost indifferent.

"That's it? *I see?* Connie, for Pete's sake, get back here."

"I can't right now, Helen. Prudence still needs me."

"Jud needs you, too, Connie."

Connie closed her eyes. She was so tired. It had been a grueling week. First the endless flights to get to New York, with her leg aching constantly. Then dealing with Prudence—gravely ill, but not nearly as bad as Vincent had implied. And, finally, after a few short hours of sleep, Vincent himself.

Her earlier suspicions had been confirmed as soon as Prudence had been over the hump. One of the reasons Vincent had been so anxious to get her to New York was to woo her back into his camp. To woo her, and get his hands on the stock, of course.

He had been relentlessly charming, single-mindedly gracious and, when all that had failed, ruthlessly frank.

Connie was proud to remember that throughout his siege she had been unfailingly adamant in her refusal. The battle had drained her, though. She was the victor, but an exhausted one.

Now she took a deep breath. Jud didn't need her. Not the way she wanted to be needed by the man she loved.

"Helen, what Jud needs more than me is to sort out his feelings. I can't help him with that, and I'm tired of being the one who does all the giving, I really am."

Helen's gasp was explosive. "Connie," she cried, "you don't mean that—"

"Oh, but I do. It's up to Jud to decide what he wants out of life. All I can do is get on with my own. And if that isn't meant to include him, then so be it."

"But, Connie—"

"Drop it, Helen. Please. And do me one more favor..."

"Anything."

"I talked with the school superintendant over in Stevensville before I called you. I got the job, and I'll probably get back in a week or so. Helen, not a word of this to Jud."

"Okay. If you're sure."

"Positive. Will you come and meet my plane?"

"Of course I will."

"And can I stay with you and Paul for the first little while until I can find a place of my own?"

"No problem. Call, okay?"

Jud peeled out of the Millers' driveway and headed north on 93 toward Victor. He was hurting bad and sorely in need of someone he could trust, let down his guard with. There was only one person he could think to go to, feeling as he did. She might not understand, but all his life she had been steadfast.

The little house, white frame with a green-shingled roof, was neat and tidy. The woman who opened the door in answer to Jud's loud rapping had long since lost the trim shapeliness of youth, but was still handsome and unbent.

Without speaking, Jud enfolded her in a hug and let his head drop onto her shoulder. His embrace was rather awkwardly returned, no more than a hesitant pat on the back, a tentative stroke along the nape of his neck.

"Jud?" Her hands, hard and callused as a man's, pushed at his shoulders. "What is it, son?"

He was making her uncomfortable, Jud realized, lifting his head to look into his mother's weathered face, perennially tanned from a lifetime of exposure to the elements. He saw the worry in the pale blue of her eyes, but also embarrassment. He had forgotten the reticence that had always been a part of his own emotional makeup, too, no doubt due to his association with—

Hell! He pulled away and offered his mother a crooked half smile that had the effect of increasing the look of concern on her face.

"What ails you, Jud? You look awful."

She peered past him at the dog sitting at attention like a gleaming black statue on her stoop. "And whose dog is that?"

Jud stepped aside and cast a glance at Rudy. "He belongs to a—" he cleared his throat "—to a...one of the fire lookouts."

"Then what are you doing with him?"

"Well, she, uh—"

His mother was quick to cut in. "*She* is it?" Something like understanding dawned in her eyes, along with a look of speculation. "And is she the reason you're here, all down in the mouth and crying on your mother's shoulder?"

Jud heaved a sigh and rubbed the back of his neck. He shook his head. "Mom, I don't—"

"I know. You don't want to talk about it. Hurtin' and pinin', but nothin' to say. You always were muleheaded. Well." She turned to address the dog. "You might as well come in, too, so's I can close the door and keep the flies where they belong."

"Come, Rudy," Jud ordered, and Rudy seemed glad to get in out of the sun. His stub of a tail wagged.

"*Rudy.* Now there's a foolish name for an animal."

"Stands for Rudolph Valentino."

"Is that a fact?"

His mother stopped pouring lemonade from the frosted pitcher she had gone to get out of the refrigerator and studied the dog once more. "Name fits, at that. I saw the man once in a moving picture, years ago."

She chuckled, shaking her head. "'Pears your fire lookout—" she put special emphasis on the possessive pronoun "—has some humor in her, at least."

"Yeah."

Jud pulled out a chair and straddled it, at the same time removing his hat. He studied it, dangled it from one finger, idly twirled it, never seeing it at all. Instead he saw Connie skipping from rock to rock in his river, calling to him, laughing.... He'd had more real fun with her than ever before in his life. And now...

He looked at his mother, work-weary and careworn, yet proud, just as he was.

"You and Dad always struck me as an unlikely couple," he said, adding as an aside, "Thanks," when his mother set a tall glass of lemonade in front of him and took the hat out of his hands. "How'd you ever get together?"

"Our folks arranged it, more or less. Seems one owed the other money—I forget the details—and the farms were combined. Fifty-three years we had together."

She set a bowl of water down in front of Rudy, then dropped heavily into the chair across from Jud. "Darned joints, always achin' these days."

"Did you love him?"

"He was a good man in his way."

"I saw him hit you once."

"Then I probably asked for it." His mother briefly pressed her lips together and looked the way she had when he'd said something bad as a youngster. When she looked into his eyes, however, there was no trace of censure, only entreaty.

"He was a good man, Jud, believe me. I know he used to be harder on you than the other kids, but—" She bit her lip and shook her head in a helpless gesture. "He meant well. He wanted to make you strong and tough, and I guess beatings were the only way he knew how. He was a hardworking, God-fearing man—"

"Mom, did you *love* him?"

Something—pain? regret?—flickered in her eyes but was gone before Jud could really decipher it. She drew a deep breath.

"Love, the kind you're talkin' about, wasn't something I grew up expecting to find. I read that it's a rare thing, and I reckon that's true."

Jud felt a lump rise up in his throat and threaten to choke him. He swallowed hard and reached across the table to cover his mother's hand with his. He couldn't speak.

She looked down at their hands a moment, then back at Jud. Her eyes were dry. Whatever crying she might have had to do, Jud figured, had been done long ago.

"Jud," she said, "if you've found that love we're talkin' about, hang on to it, son." She wiggled her hand out from underneath his and rose. "More lemonade?"

Jud absently shook his head. *Hang on to it.* Had he let it go too easily?

Picking up his hat, he unstraddled the chair and with a one-handed twirl had it in place with the seat underneath the table.

"I'd best get going," he said.

His mother nodded. "Come by when you've got things squared away."

"You bet." He stood, irresolute, then offered a smile. "I'll see you," he said shortly, adding more forcefully to Rudy, "Come, boy."

Jud strode to the door and opened it. The dog streaked out, but Jud, on second thought, let the panel fall shut again. In three long strides he closed the space between himself and his mother. Cupping one cheek, he quickly pressed his lips to the other one.

"I love you, Mom. I guess I never told you that."

Only a slight dimming of the eyes betrayed his mother's emotional state.

"I guess you never did, at that," she said very softly. Her voice quivered just a little.

"I'll see you."

Jud was almost out the door when she called. "Jud?"

He turned, "Yes, ma'am?"

"I love you, too."

He froze, stricken, staring at his mother, who offered a tentative smile, and little by little his own smile grew out of the fullness of his emotions. He nodded to her. It was a short, sharp inclination of the head that said "Thanks" and so much more.

His heart, as he stepped out into the yard, had swelled to fill his entire chest and was racing now with a strange sense of anticipation. Savoring the feeling, he found it was not an unfamiliar one after all. He'd felt the same rushing of the blood, the same foolish urge to shout and sing every time he'd been with Connie lately. Every time he'd held her in his arms, every time they'd kissed, touched, made love.

Love.

That had been it, of course. Jud froze in the act of getting into the pickup. One foot inside the cab, the other firmly planted on solid Montana soil, he felt the earth rock and his senses reel. So now what?

...if you've found that love we're talking about, hang on to it... He heard again his mother's words, spoken in the matter-of-fact tone he'd always known, yet hearing this time the bittersweet longing it strove to conceal.

Hang on to it. Good God. He hadn't. He'd let it go, he'd let Connie get away without a fight, without once telling her how much she meant to him. It would serve him right if she'd married her husband again. It would serve him right, but, Lord, let her see what a mistake that would be.

He had to stop her. He had to go after her, drag her back, make her see...

His mind made up, Jud pulled his leg from the cab and trotted back to the house.

"Mom!" He flung the door wide. "Mother!"

"I didn't go deaf in the space of three minutes, son." His mother rose from her chair. "What has you so riled all of a sudden?"

"I've got things squared away."

"Have you? I'm glad." They exchanged smiles.

"Now all I've got to do is square things with her," Jud said, his smile slipping just a little. "How'd you like some company for a couple of days?"

"Depends on who it is. If he's dark and handsome and mannerly, why, I just might be willing to take him in."

"Thanks, Mom." Jud turned and gave a shrill whistle. "Come, boy," he called, adding as Rudy flashed by, "Best get in this house while the getting's good."

Eleven

A hundred and twenty dollars a night, Jud thought, appalled. He didn't want to buy the place. Still, he signed the register without batting an eye.

"Do you have any luggage, Mr. Halverson?" the desk clerk asked pleasantly, eyes flickering with mild curiosity over Jud's Western-style clothing.

"No. Just this flight bag. I don't plan on staying more than a couple o' nights."

"I'll have to ask for payment in advance then, sir."

Jud's eyebrows rose, but he pulled out his gold American Express card without comment. "This okay?"

"Certainly. You understand, it's nothing personal, Mr. Halverson. Hotel policy. . ."

"No problem." Jud took back his card and signed the charge receipt. The formalities over, he followed the bellman up to his room. Its window faced a gray concrete wall. Jud snorted. Cities.

He picked up the phone by the bed.

* * *

Connie was in Prudence Thurston's room. It was sun-filled and airy, thanks to floor-to-ceiling windows that opened onto the garden, and was furnished with the same understated elegance that was so much a part of Prudence herself. They had just had lunch together, a simple tossed salad for Connie, clear broth and melba toast for the patient. It was almost time for Prudence's nap.

Connie sipped the last of her tea and replaced the fragile Wedgwood cup and saucer on the tray.

"Is there anything else I can get you before I leave?" she asked the frail, white-haired woman, who was reclining on a powder-blue chaise longue.

"No." Prudence shook her head with a smile, lifting an almost-transparent blue-veined hand.

Connie caught it in both of hers, squeezing gently. "I'm going to miss you."

The old woman's smile grew bittersweet. "Don't," she said. "Look forward now, not back." Only a slight slurring of the words betrayed the stroke she had so recently suffered.

"I wish—"

"Don't," Prudence said again. "It's better this way, I know that now, and it doesn't hurt to admit it anymore. Vinnie was never the man for you, though he's not all bad, you know. I spoiled him." Her eyes closed wearily. "I should have given him that stock years ago. Without strings. He's good at business, but I thought... I always hoped..."

She broke off, and her eyes snapped open. "Never you mind, now. We'll be fine. I just wish I could be sure that you will be—out there in Montana."

"Oh, yes. I will be." Connie's reply held more conviction than she felt at that moment. In spite of all the brave things she'd said to Helen in the course of their telephone conversation three days ago, she constantly caught herself thinking of Jud. Caught herself wishing, dreaming, hoping.

Now, though, she brought herself up short and smiled reassuringly at Prudence. "I'll be more than fine, I'll be gloriously happy, teaching school and feeling useful. On top of which, my leg is much better, thanks to the tender care I got from your Nurse Dixon."

"Can I have the staff do anything else for you, dear?"

Connie pressed a kiss on the parchmentlike skin of Prudence's hand. "You've done more than enough. I'm all packed and ready to go. By tomorrow this time I should be—"

"Excuse me, Mrs. Thurston." A young woman wearing a crisp white nurse's uniform stood in the door.

"Yes, Miss Dixon? Is it time for my medication?"

"Not quite. There's a telephone call for Mrs. Mart— Sorry, I keep forgetting. For Ms. Jacobi."

Connie chuckled grimly, getting up from her chair. "And to make matters worse, Ms. Dixon, after I get my hands on a certain ranger and finish strangling him, I have hopes of changing it again. To Mrs. Halverson."

She turned to Prudence. "Pru, do you mind if I take the call in here?"

"Of course not, darling." Prudence gestured toward the ornate ivory-and-chrome telephone at her elbow. "Please."

Connie picked up the receiver with a smile of thanks. "Constance Jacobi speaking."

There followed a pause on the other end, and then an all-too-well-remembered mellow baritone asked hesitantly, "Connie? What's this Jacobi business?"

Connie bit her lip, a sudden rush of tears threatening to spill over. She blinked, sent a watery smile toward Prudence, who was blatantly eavesdropping, and sank down on the edge of the chaise.

"Jud."

Prudence Thurston's face brightened.

Connie closed her eyes and, with one hand pressed to her heart, concentrated on slowing its racing tempo. Joy and relief at hearing his voice warred with lingering vexation at the worry and grief he had caused her.

"Connie, are you there?"

"I'm here."

"Good. I thought for a minute you might've hung up. Not that I'd blame you, mind, but—God, Connie, I've been a blind fool. Don't marry him, sweetheart. Please. Come back to Montana. Come back to me and give me another chance."

"Yes, Jud, but—"

"No buts." Jud's voice firmed. Entreaty became demand. "Dammit, Connie, you told me you loved me, and I'm holding you to those words. Tell the man you've changed your mind. I'm taking you back with me."

"Back with you!" Connie exclaimed. "Jud, where are you?"

"Room 614 at the Creighton Hotel. Right here in your Big Apple."

"No." The word was hardly more than an exhalation.

"Why not? What's wrong with it?" he blustered. "Costs me a fortune. Now, are you coming here, or am I going to have to come after you?"

Connie started to laugh. She was on her feet, one hand reaching out to hold on to Prudence's delicate one. "I guess I'm coming there," she told Jud. "How does forty-five minutes sound?"

"Way too long, sweetheart," Jud replied, his voice husky, all the force and bluster gone. "But I'll be here. You can count on it."

Connie stood in the hall on the sixth floor of the Creighton Hotel, knuckles poised and heart beating in triple time. She was nervous suddenly, trembling.

The door swung wide, framing Jud, her Jud, more beautifully than any Rembrandt had ever been framed.

"Hi."

"Hi, yourself." Was that squeak actually her voice?

With a long arm, clothed in faded chambray, much as it had been the very first time Connie had seen him, he hauled her into the room.

The door fell shut, and Jud leaned back against it as if to keep it that way. Still holding Connie's arm in one hand, he pulled her close and settled the other at the small of her back. With no effort at all he closed the remaining gap between their bodies and bent his head.

And kissed her.

It was a kiss of greeting, and so much more. Jud's lips staked a claim, reaffirmed possession. They spoke of starvation and need more eloquently than mere words ever could have. They spoke of apology, but most of all they spoke of love.

Connie gave herself up to the kiss without hesitation and without holding back even a shred of her own pent-up longing. She knew they had to talk, just as Jud knew. But she also knew they both needed this first.

Jud's hands were urgent, his arousal unmistakable in its unyielding strength against the flat of her stomach. Cupping her bottom, he lifted her to fit himself more intimately against the triangle at the top of her thighs. He thrust his tongue hotly into the depth of Connie's mouth, moved it erotically over hers. A prelude to what lay ahead.

Connie never wanted the kiss to end. She matched his fervor, stoking it, fueling it with all the love she had. Too many nights lately she had tossed and turned, wondering what she was lacking, demanding from an unresponsive silken canopy the reason Jud Halverson couldn't love her. She'd known it was foolish, had told herself over and over that it was he, not she, who had the problem. Common sense had been disregarded, just as it always was when emotions ruled, when the heart, not the brain, asked the questions. When love was at stake.

All too soon Jud's hold eased, and Connie slid down to stand on her own wobbly feet once again. She felt bereft, but then he lifted his head and looked down into her eyes with an expression of such undisguised love that Connie thought she would die from it.

"Marry me, Connie," Jud murmured, lowering his forehead to rest against hers for a moment. "I was a fool to doubt you, a fool for not seeing. Forgive me, please. It'll never happen again, I swear."

He raised his head and looked at her intently. "Marry me. I need you so. I—" He stopped, swallowed, then spoke again, with a smile so tentative and sweet it curled Connie's toes. "I love you, Constance Martinelli....Jacobi... whatever your name is right now. I love you."

Connie returned his smile through a mist of tears, her hands caressing the back of his neck. "Oh, Jud. I never wanted anyone but you. I love you, too. So much."

She rose to kiss his lips, savoring their silky, moist firmness. "I'm so glad you came. I was hoping you would. I told myself that everything would be fine whether you loved me or not, that I'd go back and make a life for myself, but I was so afraid...."

"I'm sorry." The words were part of the groan that rose from the depth of Jud's chest and was swallowed by Connie when his lips devoured hers once more. He slanted his mouth across hers to more fully absorb its sweetness, framing her face with both hands.

"Will you marry me?"

"Yes." Connie's voice was a whisper, a mere breath that fanned his lips like a hot desert breeze. "Yes, Jud. Yes."

He lifted her pliant body, walked to the bed and laid her in the center of it. "Let me show you how much I love you."

Without a word, Connie held out her arms, and Jud came into them with a feeling of coming home. They kissed again, explored again and found again all the wondrous ways they could set each other's bodies and souls on fire. There was no hurry now, only a relentless need to give pleasure, to heal the hurt, to bridge the chasm that misunderstanding and blind-

ness had created between them for too many days and
nights.

They shed their clothes, seemingly without drawing apart,
and the resultant feeling of heated skin on heated skin in-
toxicated them both.

Jud shifted, and Connie lay on top of him and locked her
lips on his yet again. Each delighted in the feel of tongue on
tongue; each gloried in the tastes and textures they discovered, savoring them.

Connie reveled in her position, feeling like the aggressor
with Jud beneath her writhing body, feeling powerful and
alluring. She sought to drive him mad, to make him lose
control, to make him wholly hers—as she was his.

Her insides trembling with want and need, she raised her
upper body ever so slightly, sliding the tips of her breasts
back and forth across his broad, hair-roughened chest until
both she and Jud groaned from the exquisite sensations the
movement aroused. She delved her tongue deeply into his
mouth yet again to stroke the smooth and silky surfaces
there, to tangle with his in sensual combat. She nipped sen-
suously at his firm lips.

Jud was a willing victim and an active participant. With
one hand across Connie's shoulders and one much lower, at
the gentle swell of her buttocks, he anchored her to his superior length. How well they fit in all the crucial places.
Mouth on open mouth, chest on chest, his white-hot arousal
nestled against her pulsing, feminine core.

Each rocked their hips against the other's and imitated the
rhythm of their tongues—the rhythm of love. They grew
breathless as they kissed, wildly now, insatiably.

Heart thundering in unison with hers, Jud tore his lips
from Connie's at last and, in one swift movement, reversed
their positions. His face above her was flushed; his eyes,
sapphire-bright, were aflame.

"I love you," he said again, the words a hoarsely uttered
vow. "Forever."

"Jud." Connie arched against him, clutching his hips to urge him into the ultimate union. "Show me," she cried. "Show me *now*."

And he did. He buried his manhood of velvet and steel in the liquid heat of her, to be enclosed by walls pulsing with need and desire, gently milking as he stroked.

Connie clung to his strength as she met each thrust. Wrapping her legs around his waist, she welcomed him more deeply inside her and gloried in the pleasure they created together. They were one, as only lovers can be, moving faster and faster in harmony, reaching for the ultimate joy two people can share. And finding it in a mind-splintering release that tore moans from their lips and had them writhing in agonized ecstasy.

Sated, glued to each other by sweat-dampened skin and entwined limbs, they drowsed contently.

Later, Connie lay snuggled against Jud's chest, lazily creating whorls and swirls in the mat of hair with her fingers. She was loath to breach the dreamy silence and let the cares of the world intrude, yet she was eager to address and eradicate any lingering questions between them.

"Where's Rudy?" she murmured, pressing a kiss against his collarbone.

"He's with my mother." Jud kissed the top of her head, and his breath warmed her scalp. "You smell so good."

Connie lifted her head to look into his face. "Your mother?"

"I went to see her. To get some sense of direction, to look for something solid, something stable and enduring— I don't know. We...talked. Somehow we got closer than we've ever been before. And somehow, in the process, I came to know that I loved you." Jud searched Connie's eyes. "Do you mind? My going to her?"

"Of course not. If talking with your mother is what brought you here to me, then I'm grateful to her." She kissed his chin, reaching up to smooth a shaggy eyebrow with one finger. "I love your eyes. They're beautiful."

"Oh, God." Jud caught the back of Connie's head and kissed her with fierce possessiveness. "I love you. I'll never let you go."

"I'll never want to go."

"You've changed me," Jud said. His voice like dark velvet, he told her more about his visit with his mother.

"What is she like?"

Jud thought. "Resigned," he said at length. "That's probably the best way to describe her. Accepting of the way things are. She's had a hard life, working the farm alongside my dad. I guess hugging and cuddling, feeling like we feel about each other, isn't something she's ever had."

"How sad," Connie said softly, her own happy heart contracting with sympathy. "Was your father—"

"My father was a tyrant and a bully." The words were uttered with so much suppressed violence that Connie's head jerked up and she stared, shocked, into Jud's eyes. They were green flames in his rugged face, which was now pale and tense.

"He ruled like a dictator, worked everybody like slaves and more than once beat me within an inch of my life."

"Oh, no! Jud—"

But Jud didn't hear Connie's pain-filled exclamation. He sat up, swung his legs off the bed and began to prowl the room, gloriously naked but oblivious.

Connie let him go without protest. Sitting up, too, she wrapped both arms around her knees and hugged them close.

"He always called me Raymond," Jud said softly, almost as if he were talking to himself now. "And always in that tone of voice that said I was less than nothing to him. 'Get your lazy carcass out here, *Raymond*,' he'd yell from the yard when I was doing homework or something inside, 'fore I whup your hide.'"

Jud gave a short, bitter imitation of a laugh. "And when I got there, he'd whup me anyhow. For good measure. To help me remember my place."

Connie listened with horror, her heart aching for the battered boy Jud had been. So now she knew why he hated his first name, she thought sadly, and wished she had the power to erase his pain.

"I spent my life trying to please my father," Jud said. He stood at the window, his back to Connnie, staring out at the gray bleakness that was the view. "But I never could."

He turned, and Connie could have wept for the haunted look in his eyes. "Before you, Ruth was the only one ever told me she loved me. She was a girl I wanted to marry a long time ago, when I was barely out of forestry school. She died."

With a choked sob, Connie was off the bed and running to him. She wrapped her arms tightly around his strong body, so vulnerable in its nakedness and in his need.

"Well, I love you, and I won't die," she declared fiercely. "Not for a long time."

"Thank God." Jud lifted his arms and closed them around Connie's small form. He pressed his cheek against the crown of her head and held her to him, drawing sustenance from her love and strength from the fierce passion she so willingly offered him.

For a long time neither of them moved, but when Connie involuntarily shivered in the coolness of the room, Jud scooped her up and, keeping her clasped to his chest, crawled into bed. He lay on his back and, using one hand, pulled the covers over them both.

Connie, curled in a ball on top of him, snuggled her face beneath his bristly chin.

"You need a shave," she murmured.

Jud nudged her forehead with his nose until she tilted her head at just the angle he sought, then caught her lips in a hot, openmouthed kiss. It quickly took them to the heights.

Connie unfolded her legs and opened them, beckoning as she shifted until she lay flat against Jud's muscled length. Without words, lips and tongues too busy with sweeter pursuits, she took him into her, rocking gently. Once again they experienced the incredible joy, the boundless pleasure, their bodies could share. They felt again the oneness, cried out again their words of love. And reached again that all-pervading, blinding glory that made their union so very special.

When Jud woke, it was dark. It took him a moment to get his bearings, but bursts of song and the sound of running water quickly reminded him where he was. And of all that had passed.

Happiness made him feel almost weightless as he leapt from the bed and headed for the bathroom. And he thought, with a grin splitting his face, that this must be what they called floating on cloud nine. He couldn't remember a time when he'd felt this carefree.

Inside the bathroom steam billowed as if that same cloud were there to swallow him up. Jud stepped eagerly into its humid embrace, managed to locate the shower door and went in.

"Howdy, ma'am," he drawled when Connie jumped, squealing at his unexpected touch. "You come here often?"

She gave a low, sexy laugh and turned, making sure her breasts rubbed against him as she did.

"As often as I can, cowboy. And who can blame me?" She leaned away and boldly let her eyes travel down the length of him.

With a growl, Jud caught her to him and kissed her shower-drenched lips with lazy thoroughness. When at last they came up for air, he grinned down at her.

"You may not be too bright," he said teasingly, stroking the sleek wetness of her back and lower, "but you're one hell of a good kisser."

"What?" Connie pinched his buttock. "Me not bright? I outsmarted you, didn't I? We're getting married!"

"See?" Jud drawled, tightening his hold on her slippery form. "Like I said, not too bright." He kissed her hard, and his voice grew husky. "And that surely is lucky for me."

*   *   *   *   *

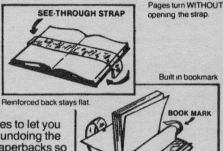

READERS' COMMENTS ON SILHOUETTE DESIRES

"Thank you for Silhouette Desires. They are the best thing that has happened to the bookshelves in a long time."

—V.W.*, Knoxville, TN

"Silhouette Desires—wonderful, fantastic—the best romance around."

—H.T.*, Margate, N.J.

"As a writer as well as a reader of romantic fiction, I found DESIREs most refreshingly realistic—and definitely as magical as the love captured on their pages."

—C.M.*, Silver Lake, N.Y.

"I just wanted to let you know how very much I enjoy your Silhouette Desire books. I read other romances, and I must say your books rate up at the top of the list."

—C.N.*, Anaheim, CA

"Desires are number one. I especially enjoy the endings because they just don't leave you with a kiss or embrace; they finish the story. Thank you for giving me such reading pleasure."

—M.S.*, Sandford, FL

*names available on request

Silhouette Desire®

COMING NEXT MONTH

#499 IRRESISTIBLE—Annette Broadrick
June's *Man-of-the-Month* is Quinn McNamara—a man with a mission. And beautiful Jennifer Sheridan has jeopardized that mission. Now only Quinn can get her out alive!

#500 EYE OF THE STORM—Sara Chance
You met Ben Forsythe in *Woman in the Shadows*. Now he's back in his own story with Cinnamon Cartier—a master at the political game but a novice at love.

#501 WILDFLOWER—Laura Taylor
Her auto accident was clearly an act of providence, and handsome widower Grayson Lennox was determined to solve the mystery of Alexa Rivers, the lovely unwed bride.

#502 THE LOVING SEASON—Cait London
A botched hotel reservation forced Diana Phillips to knock on Mac MacLean's door. The intimidating rancher seemed more concerned with his prizewinning chili than her, but not for long....

#503 MOON SHADOW—Janice Kaiser
Kira Lowell thought she had to protect her half-Indian adopted son from Joshua Bearclaw. But Joshua didn't want to take just his boy—he wanted both the woman and the child.

#504 SHARING CALIFORNIA—Jeanne Stephens
Who would have thought a basset hound could bring Annie Malloy and Sam Bennington back together? But when they inherited the canine TV star, sharing became a way of life.

AVAILABLE NOW: